"Move back, Sue," David said hoarsely.

"But, we've got to wake him—"

"I said, move back. Let me get at the blindfold."

He gripped the cloth with numb fingers and yanked it upward until it slid off the forehead and onto the ground. Then he lifted the flashlight and turned the beam straight into the man's face.

"His eyes are open," Susan breathed. "He's not asleep. His eyes are open!"

"He's not asleep," David agreed softly.

"Then why doesn't he move? Why doesn't he say something? Mr. Griffin, it's Sue—Susan McConnell—from your lit class, remember? Please, Mr. Griffin—"

David turned the light away from the wide, unblinking stare of the man on the ground beside him.

"He's not asleep," he said. "He's dead."

LOIS DUNCAN is the author of over thirty best-selling books for young people and adults. Her novels have won her high acclaim and many have been chosen as ALA Best Books for Young Adults and Junior Literary Guild selections. Her most recent novel for Delacorte Press was *Don't Look Behind You.* Among her most popular suspense stories for young people are *The Twisted Window, Killing Mr. Griffin, Stranger with My Face, Summer of Fear, Daughters of Eve, Locked in Time, Down a Dark Hall, Ransom,* and *The Third Eye,* all available in Dell Laurel-Leaf editions.

Lois Duncan is a full-time writer and a contributing editor to *Woman's Day* magazine. She lives with her family in New Mexico.

Killing
Mr. Griffin

by Lois Duncan

Published by
Dell Publishing
a division of
Bantam Doubleday Dell Publishing Group, Inc.
1540 Broadway
New York, New York 10036

To Bill and Carolyn Steinmetz

The trademark Laurel-Leaf Library® is registered in the U.S. Patent and Trademark Office.

The trademark Dell® is registered in the U.S. Patent and Trademark Office.

ISBN: 0-440-94515-1
RL: 6.0

Reprinted by arrangement with Little, Brown and Company, Inc.

Printed in the United States of America
One Previous Edition
September 1990

29 28 27 26

RAD

ONE

It was a wild, windy, southwestern spring when the idea of killing Mr. Griffin occurred to them.

As she crossed the playing field to reach the school building, Susan McConnell leaned into the wind and cupped her hands around the edges of her glasses to keep the blowing red dust from filling her eyes. Tumbleweeds swept past her like small, furry animals, rushing to pile in drifts against the fence that separated the field from the parking lot. The parked cars all had their windows up as though against a rainstorm. In the distance the rugged Sandia Mountains rose in faint outline, almost obscured by the pinkish haze.

I hate spring, Susan told herself vehemently. I hate dust and wind. I wish we lived somewhere else. Someday—

It was a word she used often—*someday*.

"Someday," she had said at the breakfast table that very morning, "someday I'm going to live in a cabin on the shore of a lake where everything is peaceful and green and the only sound is lapping water."

As soon as the words were out she had longed to snatch them back again.

"How are you going to pay the property taxes?" her father had asked in his usual reasonable way. "Lakeshore property doesn't come cheap, you know. Somebody's going to have to finance that lovely green nest of yours."

"A rich husband!" her brother Craig had shouted, and the twins, who were seven, had broken into jeers and laughter.

"Not too soon, I hope," her mother had said, turning from the stove with the frying pan in her hand. "Marry in haste, repent at leisure. That's what my grandmother always said. There's plenty of time for everything."

"For being an old maid?" the twin named Melvynne had offered, giggling.

"Don't be ridiculous," Mrs. McConnell had told him. "Nobody is ever an old maid these days. The term is 'single person.' Now, who wants eggs?"

Someday, Susan had thought, sinking lower in her chair, someday I am going to move out of this house and away from this family. I'll live all alone in a place where I can read and write and think, and the only time I'll ever come here is for Christmas.

"Are you going to be a single person, Sue?" the twin named Francis had asked with false innocence, jabbing his brother with his elbow, and Craig had grinned with maddening twelve-year-old self-assurance and said, "You've got to go out on dates before you get married, and Sue hasn't even started that yet."

"All things in good time," Mrs. McConnell had told them mildly, and Mr. McConnell had said, "On the subject of property taxes—" and they had been off on another subject.

And Susan, with her eyes on her plate, had told herself silently, someday—someday—

The dust stung the sides of her face, filling her nose and coating her lips. With a whir and a flutter, half a dozen sheets of notebook paper went flying past her like strange, white birds released suddenly from the confinement of their cage.

"Grab them!" somebody shouted. "Get them before they go over the fence!"

Susan turned to see David Ruggles running toward her, the slightness and delicacy of his bone structure giving him the framework of a kite with his blue Windbreaker billowing out beneath his arms, the wind seeming to lift and carry him. He sailed by her, grabbing frantically for the escaping papers, and Susan dropped her hands from their protective encasement of her glasses and snatched wildly at the air.

The paper she was trying for lurched suddenly to the ground in front of her, and her foot came down upon it, grinding it into the dirt. Susan stooped and snatched it up.

"It's torn!" The dirty imprint of her shoe was stamped irrevocably in its center. "I'm sorry. I'll copy it over for you."

"It doesn't matter." David shrugged his shoulders and reached to take the paper from her hand. "The rest of it's blown away anyhow. One ripped page isn't going to make any difference. If it's not all there, old Griffin won't take any of it."

"Is it a song for Ophelia?"

"Yeah. Tried to be, but Griffin would have called it something else I'm sure. I've never done anything right for him yet."

"Neither have I. Neither, I guess, has anybody."

Susan fell into step beside him, her heart lifting suddenly, her depression disappearing. The wind wasn't so bad after all, for it had blown this luck upon her, the unbelievable, undreamed-of event of herself, Susan McConnell, entering the halls of Del Norte High School side by side with beautiful, popular, elfin-faced David Ruggles, president of the senior class.

For the last year of her life, Susan had dreamed about David every night, at least every night in which she could remember having a dream. In some of the dreams he smiled at her, the open, sweet, heart-clenching smile that belonged to him alone. In others they sat and talked for hour after hour, sharing with each other private thoughts and longings. Never yet had there been a dream in which they walked shoulder to shoulder into English class with everyone, even Betsy Cline, turning to stare, to envy, to wonder.

When they reached the door to the building, David struggled with it, pulling with all the weight of his slight frame as the wind forced it closed. For a moment it seemed it would be a draw, but in the end David won, and he and Susan staggered into the crowded hallway where numerous other red-faced, wind-torn students laughed, jostled, shoved tangled hair out of their faces and shouted things like, "Great day for kite flying!" and "Look what the wind just blew in!"

Susan took off her glasses and wiped the dust from the lenses with the front of her blouse. When she put them on again David had moved away from her. She started to press forward to regain her place beside him, but others had already fallen into it. Mark Kinney. Lean. Expressionless. Cool. Jeff Garrett. Big. Loud. Broad-shouldered.

"Hey, Dave, where were you last night, man?" Jeff asked. "We looked for you after the game."

"I had to miss it. Sorry. Three hours' worth of homework."

"Two of them for Griffin's class, I'll bet."

"A lot of good that did me. Whole darned assignment blew out of my hands on the way in here—"

They were too far ahead of her now for her to hear them, and Susan accepted defeat. It didn't really matter anyway. Walking into class beside David Ruggles would have been a farce and everyone would have known it. Another girl might have pulled it off, someone with more sophistication than she, someone used to walking beside attractive boys and chatting gaily and smiling disarmingly. The only attractive boys Susan ever walked beside were named McConnell, and most of the time she hated all three of them.

Oh, well, she thought wryly, at least I stepped on his paper. That's more than has ever happened before. Next time we meet he'll know who I am—the girl with the dirty shoes. Francis's question came back to her— "Are you going to be a single person, Sue?" No. Yes. Probably—wasn't that an appropriate fate for someone like Susan McConnell, someone with a handsome father and a gorgeous, vivacious mother, whose looks had all been poured into three dreadful, handsome, smart-aleck little boys? But that was for now. Things did sometimes change. Someday—

Someday, *what?* Her boniness would blossom into curves? She would get contact lenses, she who had been told by not one, not two, but three different doctors that her corneas weren't shaped right to take contacts, even soft ones? She would turn overnight into a femme fatale? Is that what would happen?

Why did she keep trying to fool herself by thinking "someday" when the word was actually "never"?

Morosely, Susan let the tide of bodies sweep her on down the hall and to the door of Room 117. She paused in the doorway long enough to glance about the room. The boys were there ahead of her, David already in his accustomed seat, three from the back in the fifth row, Jeff blocking the center aisle as he stood by Mark's desk, continuing their conversation.

In the seat in front of David, Betsy Cline turned and said something in a low-pitched, conspiratorial manner. David smiled and nodded.

Sure that she would be unable to wedge herself past Jeff and too shy to ask him to move, Susan entered the room along the side aisle in order to approach her desk from the opposite direction. She smiled tentatively at two girls in the front of the row, but they were talking to each other and did not seem to notice her, so she let her eyes shift away from them and clung tightly to the smile, as though it had not been for them at all but for some private joke that had come suddenly into her mind. She smiled all the way up the aisle, only letting her face relax when she had slipped into her seat.

She glanced up at the wall clock at the front of the room. Two minutes to nine. Two minutes for friends to chatter to each other while Susan stared at her desk top.

Why was it that some people, girls like Betsy, for instance, were noticed and spoken to and appreciated without every making the slightest effort? It was not all looks, certainly. When you analyzed Betsy, she was not really pretty—she had a round, snub-nosed, pussy-cat face and short, muscular, cheerleader legs and a sprinkling of freckles. But ask anyone, even the newest of the freshmen, "Who is that girl over there?," and the answer you got would be, "That's Betsy Cline. Doesn't everyone know *her?*"

The large hand on the wall clock snapped forward with an inaudible click. One minute now until class time. Susan opened her purse and rummaged through it, pretending to be looking for something important. It was easier than simply sitting or than trying again with the smile routine. In other classes it was not quite as difficult. For one thing, she was a straight-A student and people had questions to ask her about homework. Here, in English Literature and Composition, there was no such thing as an A student. With all her effort she was earning B's. Even so, it was more than most of the other students were getting. The mid-semester exam had been a disaster for everyone, and it was rumored that the final was being constructed so that it would be impossible for even the brightest student to pass.

"Griffin is lying awake nights," Jeff Garrett had commented yesterday in the cafeteria. "He's trying to think of questions that don't have answers." His voice had rung through the room, and everyone had started laughing, knowing whom he was talking about, even if they had missed hearing the name.

Susan dug into the open purse and drew out a felt pen, a stick of gum, a dime and two pennies. She examined them with affected interest before letting them fall back again.

The hand of the clock moved forward one final click. The bell rang. And Mr. Griffin stepped through the doorway into the classroom, pulling the door shut behind him.

The day had officially begun.

Never once could Susan recall a morning when Mr.

Griffin had not been there standing in front of them at the precise moment the bell stopped ringing. Other teachers might saunter in late, delayed in the teachers' lounge for a last drag on a cigarette or a final swallow of morning coffee. Other teachers might pause in the hall to secure a button or tie a shoestring. Other teachers might sometimes not appear at all while unorganized substitutes stumbled over their lesson plans and finally gave up and let everybody out early.

But Mr. Griffin was there always, as reliable as the bell itself, stiff and straight in a navy blue suit, white shirt, and tie, his dark hair slicked flat against his head, his mouth firm and uncompromising beneath the small, neatly trimmed mustache.

His eyes moved steadily up and down the rows, taking silent roll as the buzz of conversation dwindled and faded to silence.

"Good morning, class," he said.

Susan answered automatically, her voice joining the uneasy chorus.

"Good morning, Mr. Griffin."

"Please take out your homework assignments and pass them to the front. Miss Cline, will you collect them, please?"

Susan opened her notebook and withdrew the sheets of lined paper on which she had carefully printed the verses she had composed the night before.

In the seat behind her, Jeff raised his hand.

"Mr. Garrett?"

"I don't have mine finished yet, Mr. Griffin. There was a basketball game last night, and I was one of the starters."

"That must have created a great problem for you, Mr. Garrett."

"I couldn't very well skip the game, could I?" Jeff

said. "The team was counting on me. We were playing Eldorado."

"Basketball is indeed an important reason for attending high school," Mr. Griffin said in an expressionless voice. "The ability to drop balls through baskets will serve you well in life. It may keep your wrists limber into old age."

"Mr. Ruggles, your hand is raised. Do you have a similar disclosure to make?"

"I did the assignment, sir," David said. "It blew out of my notebook. I'll redo it tonight."

"I have never accepted late papers on windy days. Miss Cline?"

"I didn't understand the assignment," Betsy said. Her eyes were wide and worried. "How can anybody write a final song for Ophelia when she's already said everything there is to say? All that about rosemary being for remembrance and everything? Nothing happens to her after that except she drowns."

"There are those who might consider suicide an event of some importance in a young woman's life," Mr. Griffin said dryly. "Are there any other comments?" The room was silent. "Then will those of you who were able to find some final words for poor Ophelia, please pass them forward?"

At least, we don't have to read them aloud, Susan thought in relief. That was a possibility she had not thought about last night when she sat at the desk in her room, letting the words pour from her pen onto the paper. There, caught by the magic of the painful story, she had let herself become Ophelia—lonely, alienated from the world, sickened with the hopelessness of her love, gazing into the depths of the water that would soon become her grave.

Only this morning as she was leaving the house had

the horrible thought occurred to her—what if he makes us read the songs in class? There was no way that she could have done that. Too much of Susan lay exposed in the neatly printed verses, intermixed with the person of Ophelia.

Now she scanned her words again—

> *Where the daisies laugh and blow,*
> *Where the willow leaves hang down,*
> *Nonny, nonny, I will go*
> *There to weave my lord a crown.*
>
> *Willow, willow, by the brook,*
> *Trailing fingers green and long,*
> *I will read my lord a book,*
> *I will sing my love a song.*
>
> *Though he turn his face away,*
> *Nonny, nonny, still I sing,*
> *Ditties of a heart gone gray*
> *And a hand that bears no ring.*
>
> *Water, water, cold and deep—*

"Miss McConnell, have you completed your meditation?" Mr. Griffin's voice broke in upon her.

"I'm sorry." Susan felt her face growing hot with embarrassment. "I was just—just—checking the spelling." Hurriedly she thrust the papers into the hand of the girl in front of her.

"An excellent idea, but it might have been done before now. As for those who have no paper to turn in, you may consider your grade F for this assignment. Now, open your books, please, to the first scene in Act Three."

"But, Mr. Griffin, that's not fair!" Jeff burst out.

"If we missed doing the assignment we should be allowed to make up!"

"Why is that, Mr. Garrett?"

"Other teachers take late papers!" Jeff said. "In fact, most teachers don't give assignments at all on game nights. Dolly Luna—"

"What Miss Luna does is no concern of mine. She teaches her class according to her policies," Mr. Griffin told him. "My own policy happens to be to teach English literature. If students wish to take part in extracurricular activities, that's fine, but they should be just that—*extra*. Any student who allows them to interfere with his academic responsibilities must be prepared to accept the consequences."

"And the consequences are F's, is that it?" Jeff's voice was shaking with outrage. "Well, there happen to be a lot of us who think there's more to life than trying to outdo Shakespeare! When we *do* turn stuff in, it comes back so marked up that nobody can read it. Spelling, grammar, punctuation—everything's got to be so blasted perfect—"

"Cool it, boy," Mark Kinney said quietly. He sat slouched in his seat in his usual don't-care position, his odd, heavy-lidded eyes giving him a deceptively sleepy appearance. "Jeff's sort of overexcited, Mr. G., but what he's getting at is that we're most of us seniors in this class. We need this credit to graduate."

"Darned right, we do!" Jeff sputtered. "By dumping F's out wholesale, you may be knocking a bunch of us smack out of graduation. It's not fair to us or to our parents or even to the school! What are they going to do next fall with twenty or so of us all back trying to get one lousy English credit!"

"It's interesting to contemplate, isn't it?" Mr. Griffin said mildly. "But I'd advise you not to be lulled into a false sense of security by the thought that it can't be done. I am quite capable of holding back anyone I feel has not qualified for a passing grade, a fact which your friend Mr. Kinney can support."

His hand slid into his jacket pocket and brought out a small, plastic vial. Without seeming to so much as glance at it, he snapped it open, took out a pill, and popped it into his mouth. Then he recapped the vial and placed it back in the pocket.

"Please, open your books to *Hamlet*, Act Three, Scene One. We'll now review for a quiz I have scheduled for Monday. You do have your book with you, don't you, Mr. Garrett?"

"Yes, I do—*sir*," Jeff said hoarsely.

The wind continued to blow. Gazing through the window toward the parking lot, Susan could barely make out the rows of cars, veiled as they were by swirling dust. Out of this wild, pink world a bird came flying, half blinded, carried by the wind, and crashed headlong into the windowpane. Its beak crumpled against the glass, and it seemed to hang there an instant, stunned by the impact, before it dropped like a feather-covered stone to the ground below.

Poor thing, Susan thought. Poor little thing.

Poor bird. Poor Ophelia. Poor Susan. She had a sudden, irrational urge to put her head down on the desk and weep for all of them, for the whole world, for the awful day that was starting so badly and would certainly get no better.

From his seat behind her she heard Jeff Garrett mumble under his breath, "That Griffin's the sort of guy you'd like to kill."

TWO

Well, why don't we then?" Mark asked him.

"Why don't we what?"

"Plan to kill the bastard."

"Plan to *kill* him? You mean—like—*murder?*" Jeff lowered his half-eaten hamburger from his lips without having taken the anticipated bite. "Man, you've got to be out of your head!"

The moment he heard his own voice speaking the words, he felt like an idiot. Mark had done it again. Mark had always been able to do this to him, set him up, throw out some bait, get a reaction. As long as they had known each other, since back in junior high school, Mark had played this game. Even now, at seventeen, Jeff still found himself falling for it.

"You're kidding," he said.

"You think so?"

"Well, aren't you?" He still wasn't quite certain. The times when he knew that Mark was joking, he sometimes wasn't. Here in the familiar setting of the Snack-'n-Soda Shop, amid the warmth and noise and the smell of good things frying, the word "murder" seemed totally ridiculous. Yet, this was Mark—

"Aren't you?"

"Of course, he is." Betsy set her Coke glass down on the table with a short, sharp clink. "People don't go around bumping off all their unfavorite teachers. They'd depopulate the school system. You might wish guys like Griffin would drop dead, but that's a lot different from going out and making it happen."

"You'll have to admit it would solve some problems," Mark said. "Jeff's done a neat job of lining us up for a mass flunk-out. He practically dared Griffin to do it right there in front of everybody."

"I know," Jeff said contritely. "That was dumb, all right. I just lost my temper. That asshole's been on my back all semester. He jumps me for everything. Every paragraph I write ends up looking like it's been slashed with a butcher knife."

"It's not just you," Betsy said. "He dishes it out to everybody. I've never had trouble with my other teachers. If it had been Dolly this morning, I'd have told her I hadn't understood the assignment, and she would have explained it real carefully all over again, and—"

"You two have nothing to complain about," Mark said. "I'm the one who got zapped. Last semester."

"Darned right, you did," Jeff agreed. "Right in the teeth."

"Well, it's not going to happen again, I can tell you that. I'm taking the damned course over again because I have to have the English credit to graduate. But, a third time? *No way.*"

"Never!" Betsy said. "And you shouldn't be doing it this time either. Your grades were plenty high enough for passing, even without that term paper. It was sickening what he did, the shit, making you get up in front of the class and *beg* to be allowed to retake the course."

"He can flunk you again if he wants to," Jeff said. "He can flunk us all when it comes to that. The principal will back him up, just like he did with you last time. There's not much we can do about it if he decides not to pass us."

"You suggested something when we first came in here," Mark said. "All the time we were ordering you kept sitting there muttering about how you wanted to kill the guy. Have you changed your mind this fast?"

"Now we're back where we started. You said, 'Why don't we?' And I said, 'You're kidding.' And Bets—"

"Come on," Mark said, getting to his feet. "We can't talk about this here. 'The walls have ears' and all that bit."

"But I'm not through with my Coke," Betsy objected.

"Then stay here. Jeff and I will be out in the car."

"Wait, Mark! I'm coming!" She hurriedly took a gulp and set down the half-full glass. "Who's paying?"

"Not me," Mark said. "No bread."

"I'll pay," Jeff told them. His face was hot and his heart was beginning to beat wildly. Was it possible that Mark was really serious? No, he couldn't be. To *kill* somebody? That was just plain crazy.

Still, Mark had that look about him, the one he got when he had some incredible plan in mind. It wasn't really that his expression changed; Mark had one of those faces that seldom carried any expression at all. It was a lineless face, built on a triangle with the skin stretched taut and smooth from the wide cheekbones to the sharply pointed chin. The thing that changed was the eyes. They became very bright and shiny, as though they were made of glass, and the lids slipped down over them as though to conceal the look beneath—an illusion of sleepiness.

Jeff had seen that look before, and it always meant something.

Now as they left the Snack-'n-Soda to cross the windy parking lot to Jeff's car, he felt his own excitement rising. What was brewing inside Mark's head? What was coming next?

"Okay," he said as soon as they were inside the car with the doors closed against the dust-laden wind. "Okay, let's have it. What do you have in mind? And don't tell us you're really hatching a murder plot. Betsy and I won't fall for that."

"Griffin would, I bet," Mark said quietly. "I bet we could scare the shit out of him. Nobody wants to get killed, and Griffin's no exception."

"You mean we could write him a letter and threaten him?" Betsy asked doubtfully.

"Nope. We don't want anything on paper. Besides, he'd never take that seriously. He'd think it was some kid prank. To convince him we meant business, we'd have to do it face to face."

"Go to his house and threaten him?"

"Too risky. He's got a wife, doesn't he? We don't want anybody else walking in on this. No, here's my idea—we *kidnap* him. We take him up in the mountains someplace, and we really put the screws to him. We show him what it's like for once to be the underdog, to get out from the high and mighty position behind a desk and have somebody else controlling things. We make him crawl. How's that for a scene?"

There was a moment of silence. Then Betsy said. "I don't know. It's kicky, but it sort of scares me. Kidnapping's a federal offense, isn't it? I mean, we could be arrested."

"Not if he doesn't know who we are. Not if he's blindfolded and doesn't know who's got him."

"He'd guess," Jeff said. "After that deal in class today, who do you think is the first person who'd come into his mind? Me, that's who. And you second."

"So, he guesses? What difference will that make if he can't prove anything? Most of the class hates his guts, so there are plenty of possible suspects. We're going to have witnesses who'll swear we weren't anywhere near when the thing happens."

"If there was a slipup somehow. If he did put the finger on us—"

"It wouldn't be the end of the world. We're minors, aren't we? Not one of us is eighteen yet. We're just a bunch of fun-loving kids playing a joke. Kids do that sort of thing all the time."

"You're right," Betsy said thoughtfully. "In fact, last year the senior class kidnapped Dolly Luna, didn't they? It was a kidnap-breakfast. They set it up with her roommate ahead of time and she unlocked the door for them, and they came in at dawn and grabbed Dolly in her pajamas—they didn't even let her put on a bathrobe—and dragged her out to the Pancake House. She thought it was a blast."

"They didn't threaten to kill her," Jeff said.

"If they had, and she'd reported it, would anybody have believed her?" Mark was getting irritated. "Look, if you two are chicken, just say so. There are guys in that class who would give their eyeteeth for a chance to see Griffin crawl. I can get all the help I want on this without you."

"I'm not chicken," Betsy said quickly. "I think it's a great idea. I was just worried—sort of—that we might get into some kind of real trouble. But you're right, of course. Nobody would believe him. It would sound too crazy."

"Jeff? Are you with us?"

"I guess so," Jeff said slowly. "That does make sense. I mean, like Bets said earlier, people don't bump off their teachers. He'd sound like a crackpot with a persecution complex, the kind of nut that shouldn't be teaching in the public school system." He paused. "Are you thinking of getting anybody else into this?"

"A couple of others, maybe. There's got to be a decoy, somebody who lures him into a place where we can get at him. Somebody he won't suspect of anything, even afterward. And there's got to be somebody to alibi us."

"Like who?" Jeff asked. "Greg and Tony?"

"Blabbermouth Greg? Are you kidding? We don't want *him*. And Tony's a hood. He's got a police record from that time he got caught hoisting that radio equipment. No, we want somebody above suspicion. I'd say Dave Ruggles."

Betsy frowned. "He'd never do it."

"I think he would."

"Dave's president of the senior class!" Jeff said. "He wouldn't go for something like this!"

"He'll do it." Mark spoke with certainty. "I know more about Dave than you do. He likes a challenge."

"Well, nobody would suspect *him*, that's for sure." Betsy still sounded doubtful. "He seems so straight."

"So do *you*, babe." Jeff reached over to ruffle her blond hair. "The all-American girl—head cheerleader —homecoming queen—teachers' pet."

"I'm not Griffin's pet." Betsy moved her head so that her hair slid out from under his fingers. "Okay,

Mark, I'll take your word on Dave. If you say he'll do it, he probably will. Is he the decoy?"

"No," Mark said. "I don't think he'd go for that. He wouldn't stick his neck out that far. I've got the decoy all picked out. Sue McConnell."

"Sue McConnell?" Jeff repeated the name blankly. "Who's that?"

"I know," Betsy said. "It's that junior who's taking our lit class. The little creep with the glasses. Oh, Mark, you're really too much!" She started to laugh.

"I'm not kidding," Mark said. "I mean it. She's the one."

"Why her?"

"Well, for one thing, she's a grind. You know what she got on that mid-semester test? I saw the grade when Griffin handed back the papers. It was a B. Besides that, she doesn't go around with us. Nobody would ever tie us together. You know what a decoy is, don't you? It lures things into traps by looking innocent."

"I wouldn't recognize her if you stuck her in my face," Jeff said. "Like you say, she doesn't go around with us. How do you think you're going to get her to be a part of this?"

"Dave can do it," Mark said.

"Dave? How?"

"She's got a thing for Dave," Betsy said, nodding. "Mark's right about that. It sticks out all over her. She sits in class and stares at him as if she were starving and he were a chocolate bar. It's kind of pitiful, really."

"I don't know how you can notice stuff like that," Jeff said in bewilderment. "I'm in that class too, and I can't even think who she is. Okay, I'll believe you. She has the hots for Dave. That still doesn't mean she'll be part of a kidnapping. If Griffin's giving her

B's, she's not hurting in there. For all we know she may even like the bastard."

"She doesn't," Mark said. "She's used to A's. She gets back a paper with a B or C on it and crumples it up and dumps it in the trash. She's homely and she's lonely and she's one unhappy chick. If Dave will put a little sunshine into her life, she'll give him the moon."

"What are you anyway, some kind of psychologist?" Jeff regarded his friend with undisguised awe. "How do you know stuff like that?"

"I watch people. I notice things."

Jeff thought of Mark in class, sitting silent in the seat behind him, regarding everyone and everything from beneath those heavy, half-closed lids—studying faces, analyzing expressions, drinking in details and storing them away in the iron-gray filing cabinet of his mind. "I guess you must."

He remembered the first time they had met each other. Jeff had been twelve then, big for his age, standing head and shoulders above the others in the seventh-grade classroom. He had felt huge and self-conscious. His voice had already been starting to change. When roll was called he had answered with a froglike croak, and the rest of the class had burst into laughter.

Even the teacher had smiled, and Jeff had felt the sting of hot tears in his eyes. He had blinked them back, furious at himself, hating all of them. Choking on his own fury, he had wedged himself into the seat behind his desk, wishing he could disappear beneath it.

His eyes had shifted sideways, and he had found himself caught by the gaze of the boy in the seat across from him. He was a strange-looking boy with a face like a fox and cool, appraising, gray-marble eyes.

The boy had continued to stare at him without a flicker of anything that looked like honest interest. He had just stared. Jeff had dropped his own eyes. A few minutes later he had raised them again. The boy was still staring.

When lunch period arrived, Jeff had stayed in his seat, pretending to shuffle through papers until the classroom was empty. Then he had gotten up and gone out the door into the hall.

The boy had been standing there, waiting for him.

"You get mad too easy," he had said, falling into step beside him. "You let everything hang out. That's not good."

"What's it to you?" Jeff had asked angrily. "Who the hell are you, anyway? I've never seen you around before."

"My name's Mark Kinney. I'm new in town. Moved here to live with my aunt and uncle." The boy had been a good six inches shorter than he, but he walked tall. Jeff had the strange feeling that they were the same height. "You're Jeff Garrett."

"How do you know that?"

"I listened at roll call. I remember names." The boy's shorter legs had lengthened their stride to keep pace with Jeff's longer ones. "I'm gonna do something after school. Something real interesting. Want to come?"

"What?" Jeff asked, interested despite himself. "What are you going to do?"

"Do you like cats?"

"Not especially."

"Neither do I. I've got a plan. Something I'm going to do with a cat. You coming?"

"Will it take long?" Jeff had asked. "I've got a paper route."

"Not long."

"Okay, I'll come then." He had looked at the boy more closely now, at the odd, wide-cheeked face, the tight, tan skin, the sparkling gray eyes. There was something almost magnetic about those eyes. "What are you going to do?"

"You'll see."

"Where are you going to do it?"

"Behind the school. Behind the cafeteria where they keep the garbage cans. I'll meet you there at three-thirty."

"Okay. Why not?" He did not know why he agreed. He had no real interest in meeting anybody anywhere when school was over. But he had said, "Okay." And he had gone.

Now, five years later, he heard himself saying again, "Okay. Okay, why not?"

"Good boy," Mark said, and Betsy flashed him a smile of approval. Jeff slid his hand along the back of the seat until it rested behind her head. This time she did not pull away.

"It'll be fun," she said. "Like a game. We ought to have *something* fun to remember from high school. When my dad was in school, do you know what *he* did? He and a friend of his got a copy of a key to one of the doors of the building, and one night they took a horse out of a farmer's pasture and put it in the girls' restroom. He still talks about it—the way a bunch of girls went in the next morning and came screaming out!"

"We'll remember this the same way," Mark said. "You'll tell your kids about it. Griffin, thrashing and crawling, begging us not to hurt him—that'll be something to remember, all right."

He wasn't smiling. Mark seldom smiled. But his face

was aglow with a strange luminosity, an inner light that seemed to come through his skin and give it an odd, ethereal radiance. His eyes, what could be seen of them under the drooping lids, had the glint of smoked glass caught in a ray of sunlight. No one would ever have called Mark Kinney handsome, but there were moments when he had a special beauty, something so striking and strange that it stopped the heart and caused those near him to catch their breath.

It was a transformation Jeff had come to recognize. He had seen it for the first time back in junior high school, on that day they had met each other—the time that Mark had set fire to the cat.

THREE

Davy, is that you, dear?"

"Yes, Gram. Who else?"

"Aren't you going to come in to see me?"

"Sure. Just a sec." David finished spreading mustard on a slice of bread, laid a hunk of cheese on it, and doubled it over. Picking up the sandwich with one hand and a glass of milk with the other, he left the kitchen and walked through the small, dark living room into the bedroom beyond.

The old lady was in her accustomed place in the armchair by the window, the spot from which she could look directly across into the bedroom window of the house next door. She was wearing her blue flowered housecoat, and her long hair was pulled back and held in place with a blue ribbon, so that it fell, limp and gray, over the slanted shoulders and down the back in the style of a teenage girl.

"So, an after-school snack is more important than coming in to say hello to your grandmother?"

"Not usually, Gram. Today I missed lunch." David

crossed the room and leaned over to place a dutiful kiss on the pink, rouged cheek. The skin felt cool and dry to his lips, and so soft that it seemed to sink beneath the pressure of the kiss and lie there, indented. "What have you been doing today?"

"What do I ever do? Watch the game shows. A lady today from Kansas City had to guess something behind a curtain that cost five thousand dollars. What do you think it was?"

"Any clues?"

"The man—the one who asks the questions—he told her, 'It runs.' "

"A car?" David guessed.

"That's what she thought, but it turned out to be a racehorse, can you imagine? Did you ever think a horse would be worth that much money? The poor lady didn't get anything except some little consolation prize like a hair dryer or something. It doesn't seem fair, does it? They kept saying things to make her think it was going to be a car."

"Well, that's how it goes, I guess."

"But it wasn't fair." The weak old eyes settled upon David's sandwich. "What is it you have there, Swiss cheese? That does look good."

"Would you like me to make you one?"

"Well, maybe just a half. Your mother went off to work this morning and didn't bother to leave anything fixed for my lunch, only a little bit of tuna. She didn't even leave a Jello-O. I know we have some. I saw the package last night when she brought it home from the grocery."

"I'll make it up. If I do it now, it'll be jelled by dinner."

"Make up the green. It's got the most flavor."

"The green it will be."

He left the bedroom and went back to the kitchen. The remains of the sandwich makings were spread out on the table, and he eyed them carefully, wondering if he had left enough cheese for the promised sandwich. Deciding that he had not, he took some out of his own and replanted it between two fresh slices of bread. He put a pan of water onto the stove to boil and opened the cabinet where his mother stored foodstuff. There were two boxes of Jell-O, cherry and banana.

"Good old Mom," he muttered resignedly. "She bought everything but green."

There were times when he wondered if his mother did this sort of thing deliberately, knowing that the old woman liked lime Jell-O and knowing too that he would be the one stuck with telling her that it wasn't there.

As soon as he allowed such a conjecture to cross his mind, he was swept with guilt. His mother did well to make it to the grocery store at all after a full day taking dictation and typing. In her place another woman would have forgotten the Jell-O completely, or maybe even not have come home at all. There were women who did that, just took off and went when things got too rough for them. He had read an article on that subject only recently. The author had given some startlingly high number of such cases and had said that runaway wives in America were soon going to equal or exceed the number of runaway husbands.

But his mother would not be one of them, of that he could be sure. To begin with, she wasn't a wife and hadn't been one for over ten years. On top of that, she was superresponsible. Everybody told him that—his aunts, the neighbors, even their minister.

"I hope you appreciate your mother," the Reverend Chandler had said one Sunday after services. "There aren't many women who would do what she has— taken an invalid mother-in-law into her home to love and care for after being deserted by her own husband. Your mother's a saint, son, and don't you forget it. You're a lucky boy to have the opportunity of growing up in her home."

"I know it, sir," David had assured him, conscious of his mother standing behind him, knowing without looking that she had heard the minister's words and was pleased by them.

When they reached the car she had been smiling a little and the harsh lines between her eyes and at the corners of her mouth had softened. At that moment she had looked startlingly like the girl in the wedding picture that David had found one day in a suitcase in the attic.

"Would you like to stop and pick up some ice cream on the way home?" she had asked him.

The pleasant mood had stayed with her most of the rest of the day.

"Davy?"

"Coming, Gram. I've got your sandwich." He carried it in to her on a plate. "Do you want some milk?"

"No. It curdles in my stomach. That's what happens when you get old. Have you made the Jell-O?"

"I'm getting ready to now."

Back in the kitchen he poured the boiling water into a bowl and mixed in the banana gelatin and added ice. He set the bowl in the refrigerator and ran more water into the sink over the breakfast dishes. He dumped in detergent.

David Ruggles, President of the Senior Class, King of the Sink! His lips curled wryly. What would the kids at school think if they could see him now?

David had never overestimated himself. He knew

exactly who he was and what he could do with what he had. He knew he was handsome. It was an unusual sort of handsomeness, but it was there, and it worked.

He looked exactly like his father. He couldn't remember his father very well, but he knew what he looked like from the wedding picture. His father had been a small man, slightly built, with the most beautiful face in the world. When David looked at himself in the mirror he saw that face looking back at him, fine boned, delicate, perfectly shaped with gentle eyes and a fine, sensitive mouth.

He wondered sometimes what his father had been like as a person, with a face like that. He compared the face with his mother's, strong and sensible, and he tried to imagine the two of them together, laughing and joking and holding hands, kissing perhaps. It was impossible. In his mind his father's face was floating on a cloud, his mother's coming in the door behind a bag of groceries. One was a dream, the other reality.

He finished sponging the dishes and ran hot water from the tap straight over them to wash off the suds. His mother didn't like him to do this as it used up too much hot water, but it was fast and easy.

From the back room his grandmother called, "Davy? Is the Jello-O ready yet?"

"No, Gram. It'll be a couple of hours. I just put it in the fridge."

He left the kitchen and went in to pick up the sandwich plate.

"Do you need anything more?"

"Yes," the old woman said. "I have to go to the little girls' room."

"Oh, Gram, can't you wait awhile?"

"I've been waiting all day."

He knew this was not true. There was no way his

grandmother waited all day for something like that. When she was alone in the house, she got up and did whatever it was she had to do. He knew for a fact that she went to the refrigerator and took out the lunch his mother left prepared for her, and there were times when he found things around the house—candy, movie magazines—that must have been purchased down at the corner store.

But now, helpless in the flowered bathrobe, she appealed to him.

"I have to go."

"All right, Gram. Okay. Hold on to me."

He helped her out of the chair and, slipping one arm around her scrawny body and a hand beneath her elbow, he half led, half carried her to the little bathroom that sat between the bedroom and the kitchen.

"You okay now?"

"All right, Davy. I'll tell you when I want to go back."

"You do that." His voice was sharp. He caught it and forced a gentler tone. "You call me, Gram." That was better. "I'll be right here."

He went into the living room, a dark, small room with a musty smell. He had often wondered why it was called a "living room," since it seemed to have less life than any other room in the house. The blinds were usually drawn to protect the rug from the morning sun, and they were seldom raised in the afternoon because no one thought to raise them. The couch was covered with a plastic casing. The books and radio were in his room, the television in the room shared by his mother and grandmother.

The only thing alive in the whole living room was the telephone, and it sat silent on its hook so much of the time that it might as well not have existed at all.

He sat down next to it and considered dialing a number. Any number, just to hear a voice. He could call Mark—but no, Mark was never home in the afternoons. He would be out somewhere with Jeff and Betsy, or some of the rest of the group that always trailed around after him. What they did when they "went out somewhere" was never exactly explicable. Most of the time they just rode around in Jeff's car, stopping at one place after another, wandering aimlessly about town, honking the horn at friends and laughing and kidding around.

He knew he was welcome to join them. Mark had asked him more than once, and Jeff had also.

David had said, "Thanks, but I've got stuff to do at home," and let it go at that. He knew they would never understand his mother's reasoning that there should be a definite, preplanned activity or time was being wasted.

"Where is it you're going?" she would ask. "What is it you're going to do there? Where can I reach you in an emergency?"

It wasn't that she forbade him to go places, it was just that by the time they finished hashing things over his enthusiasm had usually faded to the point where going was hardly worth the effort.

"Unless there's a reason," his mother said, "a real reason, it's nice for you to be at home in the afternoons. Your grandmother sits there alone all day, you know, and your homecoming at three is the high point of her day."

In the evenings they ate later than most people because his mother wasn't up to facing the kitchen immediately after a day at work.

Then there was homework.

"It's important to keep up with your studies," his mother told him. "You're our hope for the future, Davy. Anything good that happens to this family will come through you."

This was true, he knew, and he thought about it often. His mother's salary as a secretary was not going to increase, and there was no place she could move within the ranks of the company for which she worked. Unless she remarried, her life was at a stalemate, and remarriage for her seemed highly unlikely. It wasn't that she was unattractive; at forty-two she still looked remarkably good, with a lean, strong figure and hair as dark and thick as David's own. But she had no interest in meeting men or in going out with them.

"One marriage is enough for anybody," she stated firmly. And then, after a slight pause, she would sometimes add, "More than enough," with a note of bitterness in her voice.

So when David was grown, his mother would be there still, slaving away to make ends meet. And for all he knew Gram would be there too. For an invalid, Gram seemed amazingly healthy, scarcely ever coming down with the illnesses other people were prone to. Perhaps it was because, cloistered as she was, she never got exposed to any germs. Anyway, despite her age, she didn't show any indication of leaving her present world for the next one at any time in the near future.

When he hit the job market, David figured, he could count on two people to support other than himself. For that reason it was important to have the best educational background possible. His father had gone to Stanford. That, for David, was out of the question, but with a top-notch transcript and high A.C.T.

scores, he figured he would definitely be in the running for the special scholarship offered annually by the president of the University of New Mexico to an outstanding and needy student from the Albuquerque area. In the long run, he had his hopes pinned on law school. To this end he ran for school offices and took part in debating and other speech-oriented activities. Such things looked good on your record if you were aiming for a prelaw program.

Now, in his last semester of high school, that record looked good, but since the president's scholarship was not awarded until final grades were out, what concerned him was the upcoming grade in English. He had always considered himself a good English student; he read his assignments faithfully and was meticulous about his essays. Dolly Luna, last year's teacher (formally she was "Miss Luna," but the first day of class she had told them, "Call me Dolly"), had given him A's on all his papers, followed by strings of exclamation marks.

But the same sort of essays submitted in Mr. Griffin's class brought C's.

"Mechanics okay," Griffin had written on one paper. "You have a grasp of grammar and punctuation, but the writing itself is shallow. There's nothing to it. Don't parrot back my lectures. Get under the surface. Tell me something about Hamlet I don't already know."

"Something he doesn't know!" David had exclaimed in frustration when that paper was returned to him. "He's supposed to be the expert. I'm just a student. If there's stuff about Shakespeare he doesn't know, what's he doing teaching it?"

And now, today, those blown-away papers added an F to his grade list, which very likely brought the average down to D. He had done what he could about it, even to skipping lunch in order to rewrite the paper, but true to his word, Griffin would not accept it.

"I thought I made it clear, Mr. Ruggles," he had said in his cool, crisp voice, "that I do not take late papers, no matter what the excuse for them may be."

So that whole hour's work had gone for nothing, and unless he could ace the final, which seemed unlikely, he would probably find that D permanently situated on his transcript.

"I can see why Mark did what he did last semester," he muttered angrily. "I might be tempted to try the same thing myself, if I thought it would do any good."

The doorbell rang.

Startled, David reached for the telephone receiver, stopped, waited. Yes, it had been the doorbell.

Who on earth, he thought, getting up and crossing the room.

He opened the front door.

"Oh, hey, I was just thinking about you."

"You were, huh?" Mark's lean figure stood slouched in the doorway. "You got a chick in there or something? Why's it so dark?"

"You know my mom," David said. "She doesn't want the rug to bleach out. You got the gang with you?"

"Jeff and Betsy are out front in Jeff's car. Want to go cruising? We've got an idea about something we want to talk over with you."

"I can't right now. I've got stuff I'm supposed to be doing here." David was acutely conscious of the old woman in the bathroom only a couple of yards away. Any moment now her voice might ring out asking to be taken back to her room.

Mark knew more about his family life than anyone

at school, but details like this were more than he needed to be subjected to.

"I'll walk out to the car with you," David said. "Can't you cue me in on the basics?"

"It'll take more time than that," Mark said. "There's a lot to be worked out. What it boils down to is this—we're out to work over old man Griffin."

"Work him over?"

"Scare him shitless. Get him crawling. Teach him he can't pull the sort of stuff he pulled today."

"How are you going to do it?"

"We're going to kidnap him," Mark said. "We're going to make him think we're going to kill him."

"Oh, wow," David said, drawing in his breath. "That's heavy stuff, man. You could get into all kinds of trouble."

"I don't think so. Not if he's blindfolded. Not the way I'm working it out." Mark put a hand on his shoulder. "How about it, Dave? Want to be a part of it?"

From the dark behind them a cracked old voice called, "Davy?"

"Look," David said, "like I told you, I've got some stuff to do. Later, after dinner, I'm going to the library. I'll meet you then, say around eight, okay? At the Snack-'n-Soda?"

"Not okay. I need to know *now*." Mark's hand remained warm on his shoulder. His voice dropped until it was almost a whisper, so intense that the words came forth in short, painful jabs. "Dave, boy—how can you stand it—living like this? How long has it been—since you did something crazy—just for the hell of it? How long has it been—since you've done something wild— just for fun?"

"You're not really planning to hurt him?"

"Hell, no. Just scare him. Shake him up some. Are you with us?"

All of David's life rose up behind him in one great, gray wave.

"Count me in," he said.

FOUR

It was the sound of the telephone ringing in the upstairs hallway that woke Susan at nine-thirty on Saturday morning. She was always aware of the telephone;
it was situated directly outside her bedroom door.

Who can be calling so early, she thought irritably,
squirming over onto her stomach and burrowing her
face into her pillow to escape the sunlight that was
streaming between the half-drawn curtains and flooding the room with unwelcome brilliance.

Saturdays were special to Susan. They meant that
she did not have to get up in time to sit through the
ordeal of a family breakfast with all the squabbling
and spilling and teasing that went with it. She did not
have to go to school and smile her way through a
morning filled with semistrangers; she did not have to
worry about which cafeteria table to sit at during
lunch and whether to tack herself onto the edge of a
group that was already eating or to sit alone and wait
to see if someone sat down beside her.

On Saturdays she could sleep late and get up at last to a house with most of the people already out of it. She could make herself peanut butter toast and read at the table, and after that she could shut herself back in her bedroom and write. She could spend her whole day there if she wanted to, unless, of course, her mother dragged her out to do some household chore.

The telephone had no right to ring on Saturday mornings. People should tiptoe softly about, not disturbing each other. The boys should tell their friends that if they wanted to see them they could stand in the yard and toss pebbles at their windows, not bring the house down with the shrillness of a telephone blast.

Why doesn't someone answer it, Susan thought as the phone continued to ring. Are they deaf or are all of them out somewhere?

Finally, with a sigh of resignation, she dragged herself out from under the covers and crossed the room to the door. Her hand was on the knob when the ringing stopped.

Craig's voice called, "Sue! It's for you!"

"For me?" Susan turned the knob and stepped out into the hall. "Who is it?"

"How should I know? Some guy." Craig's voice was on the edge of changing. Sometimes it came out high and shrill like a little boy's, and the other times it started deep and ended in a creak. Now it was suddenly very low and almost booming. "Don't tell me the single person's got herself a boyfriend!"

"Oh—hush. She snatched the receiver from his hand. "Hello?"

"Hello, Sue?" a masculine voice said. "This is David Ruggles."

It's a joke, Susan thought. It's something Craig and the twins have rigged up for me.

"David who?" she asked, trying to keep her voice steady.

"It's Dave Ruggles, from school. From your lit class. The one whose papers you were chasing yesterday, remember?"

"Oh, yes. Yes, of course, I know who you are." It was not a joke then; it was real. Or perhaps she was still in bed asleep and dreaming.

"It's such a neat day out," the voice on the telephone was saying, "with the wind down and everything, a bunch of us thought we'd take a picnic up into the mountains. I was wondering if you might like to go."

"You mean, today?"

"Well, sure, today. Are you busy?"

"No," Susan said. "I'm not busy at all. I'd like to go."

"You would? Great. We'll be by for you around eleven then. Okay?"

"Okay," Susan said. And then, as a frantic afterthought, "Do you know where I live?"

"The address in the phone book is right, isn't it?"

"Yes. Yes, it's right. Okay, then, I'll see you in a little while."

Stunned, she replaced the receiver on the hook. For a moment she simply stood there, staring at it, at the pale beige plastic instrument that had brought the incredible message.

"*I have a date.*"

"You're kidding," Craig exclaimed with astonishment. "That guy really asked you out?"

"To a picnic."

"Cripes! Wait till I tell the twins!" With a bellow of laughter, Craig went rocketing down the hall, shouting his piece of news.

Susan went back into her room and shut the door.

I have a date with David, she told herself numbly. She could say the words, but she could not actually believe them. She went into the bathroom and brushed her teeth. The face in the bathroom mirror looked back at her, softly blurred because she was not wearing her glasses. It was a rather narrow face with a high forehead, and it was framed with fine, mouse-colored hair. It was *not* the face of a girl David Ruggles would ask for a date.

Yet, it had happened—it had happened.

She rinsed out the toothbrush and hung it on the rack and went back into her room and got dressed. Jeans and sandals and a green, tie-dyed T-shirt. She combed her hair and put on her glasses, and the room came into focus.

I have a date with David!

There was a brief, perfunctory knock. The bedroom door opened and her mother came in.

"Craig told me the news!" she said. "My goodness, Sue, who is this boy?"

"He's the president of the senior class!"

"And you're only a junior! How exciting!" Her mother's eyes were shining. "What are you going to take?"

"Take?"

"Craig said it was a picnic."

"I didn't think about that." Susan regarded her mother blankly. "What'll I do? I don't know what other people are bringing. He didn't say anything about the food."

"I'll make you some sandwiches," Mrs. McConnell said. "We have chicken left over from last night's dinner. And there's still some chocolate cake; at least, I think there is, if the boys haven't eaten it. Does that sound all right?"

"I guess so," Susan said. The numbness was beginning to wear off now, and she felt the sharp edge of panic rising within her. "Oh, Mother, what if it's awful? I mean, what if I can't think of anything to talk to him about?"

"Just talk about the same things you talk about at school."

"We don't talk in school. He doesn't sit near me in any classes. I talked to him yesterday, just for a minute, about the lit assignment, but that's not the kind of thing you say twice. I mean, we talked about that, and now it's done. You can't keep discussing an assignment."

"You'll think of something. That's the sort of thing that takes care of itself. He'll probably have things *he* wants to talk about. He must like you, honey, or he wouldn't have called."

I have a date with David!

At eleven-ten the doorbell rang, and he was there. Handsome and smiling, unselfconsciously shaking hands with her parents, reaching out to take the handle of the picnic basket.

"Don't worry, Mrs. McConnell, she'll be safe. Jeff Garrett's driving, and he's really careful."

Even Craig's curious inspection and the snaggle-toothed leers of the twins didn't appear to faze him. Susan stared at his hands. They were the cleanest hands she had ever seen, long and slender with tapering fingers. She was afraid that if she lifted her eyes and looked him full in the face, she would be blinded as though she were looking straight into the dazzling radiance of the sun.

"Have fun," her mother said.

"Don't eat too much," came from her father, who did not seem to understand the significance of what was happening, that his sixteen-year-old daughter was finally, at long last, about to embark on a first date, and that it was not just any boy who had asked her out but this particular boy.

They crossed the lawn to the car, and David opened the door for her and lifted in the basket.

"You know everybody, don't you? Jeff—Mark— Betsy."

"Hello, Sue! What a cute shirt! Did you dye it yourself?" Betsy Cline threw her a warm, bright, welcoming smile.

"Hi, Sue," Mark said, and Jeff said, "Great day for a picnic, right? It's almost like summer."

And that suddenly—that easily—she felt she was one of them.

Her mother had been right, there was no problem with talking, because the rest of them were talking so much themselves. They seemed to know each other well, but not so well that they excluded her from their conversation. With everything that was said, a door was opened deliberately so that she could enter with a comment. They drove out of the city on the freeway and turned off onto the paved road that led to the mountains, and almost immediately the fresh green of the spring trees surrounded them and the sky arched blue above their heads.

Mark opened a six-pack of beer.

"If it were pop, it would look like a TV commercial," he said, and they all laughed, Susan right along with them. She had never thought of Mark as being funny before. In fact, she had always been a little frightened of him, with his smooth, expressionless face and knowing eyes. But now, suddenly, he wasn't frightening at all—just gay and carefree—and it *was* like a TV commercial with a car full of beautiful, laughing, young people setting out to spend a day together in the hills.

After several miles Jeff turned again, and this time they were on a dirt road that curved and twisted and doubled back upon itself until it seemed to be going nowhere.

At last they came to a clearing and Jeff stopped the car and they all got out.

"This is the place," Mark said. "Lana and I used to come up here all the time. You can't see it from here, but there's a path over there by that rock and it leads to a waterfall."

He began to lead the way, and the rest of them fell into step behind him, walking Indian file, David carrying the picnic basket and Jeff with a blanket and a brown paper sack of food that Betsy had brought.

Susan followed along in David's footsteps, his slim, straight back moving directly ahead of her. They walked through the woods, and it was still—there was nothing but the sound of their feet crunching dead branches.

"Who's Lana?" she asked David in a low voice.

"The girl Mark used to go with—until Griffin gave it the ax. You've heard about that, haven't you? I thought everybody had."

"I haven't."

"Well, I'll tell you later." He tossed her a smile over his shoulder.

I've dreamed this before, Susan thought. I wrote about it later and pretended it really happened once when Mr. Griffin wanted a descriptive essay. He said I picked nice adjectives, but he marked me down for spelling.

They heard the waterfall before they saw it. The closer they got, the louder it became, until they broke through the trees and were upon it, a frothing, tumbling, churning burst of silver that poured itself madly over rocks and then dropped straight down for several feet into the stream below.

"Hey, far out!" Jeff exclaimed, and Betsy gave a little squeal of delight.

"I didn't know it was back here!"

"Nobody does," Mark told her. "Nobody ever comes here. Lana and I stumbled on it one day when we were out hiking. We came back a lot of times, and we were the only ones."

"Neat, huh?" David said, smiling at Susan.

"It's simply beautiful!"

She felt she should say something more, but the words wouldn't come, and anything she made herself say would be too little or too much.

"Let's eat!" Jeff said. "I hope you chicks brought plenty of food. I'm starving!"

"Aren't you always?" Betsy said with a laugh. "You guys are all bottomless pits."

They spread the blanket on the ground and ate their lunch on the bank of the stream on the very edge of the sparkling water.

Afterward they lay stretched out on the blanket and on the grass and talked in an easy, lazy manner as if they had all been friends forever. Mark was leaning against the trunk of a tree, smoking a joint, and the sweet, heavy scent of pot blended with the incense of the sun-soaked pine needles. Betsy was lying on the blanket, her blue-jeaned knees drawn up into little pointed peaks. Her eyes were closed, and she looked totally at peace. Jeff was sprawled next to her, on his back. He was dreamily studying the line of a pine branch stretching squarely over his head.

Susan took off her glasses and laid them on her stomach, and the world went soft and unfocused around her.

"You look different without your glasses," David said softly. "Your whole face changes. Do you really have to wear them?"

"Only if I want to see," Susan told him, amazed at her sudden ability to answer such a question lightly. "It helps when you're walking and stuff. You know—so you don't bump into things."

"You look okay with them on," David said. "It's just that now—with them off—you look so sort of fragile. Like you need to be taken care of or something."

"I wonder what Mr. Griffin looks like without *his* glasses," Betsy said. She spoke without opening her eyes. "Fragile? Like he needs to be taken care of?"

"Are you kidding?" Jeff started to laugh. "We'll have to take them off before we blindfold him. We don't want to shove them straight through his eyeballs."

"Blindfold him?" Susan thought she had heard him incorrectly. "Did you say *blindfold?*" Suddenly, she realized that the atmosphere had changed abruptly. The blurred ovals of their faces were turned toward her. Waiting. Calculating.

"You heard right," Jeff said slowly, and they told her the thing that they were going to do.

Later Susan could not recall exactly which one told her or whether they all did, each speaking a part, the voices overlapping and running together like the lines and curves of David's face as he raised himself on one elbow and leaned over to touch the tip of her nose lightly with one finger.

"You like our idea?"

"You're kidding me. You're not really going to do
t."

"Damned right we are."

"I don't believe you. It's like something out of a
ook." She could accept it when she thought of it that
vay, as a story, the people in it characters created by
n author. She could imagine the words neatly printed
n a page: "The shadowy figures seized him from be-
ind and forced him into the waiting car. His cries for
elp brought no response. Where were they taking
im? What were they going to do?"

"It's unreal," she said. "You're making it up to tease
ne."

"You can be in on it if you want to."

"Me? How?" Susan asked.

"Mark will tell you. He's doing the planning."

"You can make an appointment with him for after
chool," Mark said. "Pretend you want to talk with
im about the term paper or something. Hold him till
he grounds are empty. Then, when he walks out to
he parking lot, we'll get him."

"You really think it would be that simple?"

"Sure. Why not?" Mark took a long drag on the
joint and let the smoke curl slowly from between his
teeth. "The best things in life are simple. Simple
things work. They don't foul up. It's the complicated
things that get twisted around on you."

"We'll all have our parts," Betsy said. "Mine will be
to provide alibis for everybody. The fellows are going
to blindfold Griffin so he won't be able to see who
anybody is. Then afterward he won't be able to accuse
anyone."

"He'll know *me* if I make the appointment," Susan
said. "He won't be blindfolded then."

"He won't even guess you're part of it," Mark told her easily. "It'll just seem like a coincidence. He stays after school to talk with a student, he goes outside and we're waiting for him by his car. You'll have split before that happens. You won't even be on the scene."

"But why?" Susan asked. "What's the reason for it all? People don't get kidnapped without a reason."

"The reason is that he deserves it," Mark said sharply. "Does there have to be any other reason than that? He's an asshole. He's out to flunk all of us. Maybe if we shake him up a little he'll get off this power trip of his and start treating us like human beings."

"I don't know," Susan said hesitantly. "I've never been mixed up in anything like this."

"Who has?" Jeff said. "It'll be a first time for all of us. My God, we've got to do something really wild once in our lives before we're grown and tied down. Let's get some kicks while we can, and we'll teach old Griffin a lesson at the same time."

"When would you want to do it?"

"What about Thursday?" Mark said. "That will give us time to get all the details worked out. Besides, he's giving a quiz Monday, which means we'll probably get the papers back Wednesday. That way you could call him Wednesday night and ask him for a conference after school the next day. You could say you want to discuss the test."

"Okay, Sue?" David asked.

"Well—"

"Come on."

"Okay." She heard her voice speaking the word, and her heart rose suddenly into her throat. Had she really said that? Had she actually agreed to this insanity?

"Good for you!" Jeff said, and Betsy gave a crow of pleasure.

"I knew you'd do it, Sue!" she said. "I told the guys."

"That's my girl," David said softly, and he kissed her. Lightly. On the forehead. His lips were like the touch of butterfly wings.

Never, Susan thought deliriously, never in all the time to come will I ever, ever be as happy as I am right now.

And she was right.

FIVE

The alarm went off at seven, and Kathy Griffin reached out without opening her eyes and pressed the button to shut it off. Just as automatically, she reached for Brian in the bed beside her, to find nothing but an empty pillow and a mass of tangled bedclothes.

She groped for a moment, as though expecting to find him there, twisted somehow into the sheets or buried beneath the untidy lumps of blanket. Then, as she became more fully conscious, she sighed and opened her eyes to affirm the fact that she was, indeed, alone in the double bed.

That man, she thought. I don't know why he owns an alarm clock. He never bothers to use it.

The sound of running water told her the shower in the bathroom was in use. She lay quiet, letting herself come slowly awake, until the water stopped and she heard the shower stall open and slam closed.

A few moments later the bathroom door opened,

and Brian came into the bedroom, dressed in T-shirt and undershorts, toweling his hair.

" 'Morning, Bri," Kathy greeted him, hauling herself to a sitting position. "What's the order of the day, fried or scrambled?"

"Go back to sleep," Brian told her. "I'll fix my own eggs this morning."

"No, that's my job." A moment before she would have given anything to have been able to roll over and sink back into slumber. Now that she had been given permission, some contrariness in her personality kept her from doing it. She swung her legs over the side of the bed and stood up slowly, adjusting herself to the unaccustomed weight of her rounded belly.

"There's nothing in the rules that says that pregnant women can't cook breakfast."

"You're sure you feel like it?"

"Of course." And now, suddenly, she did. She gave him a quick kiss on the cheek in passing, pulled a terry-cloth robe on over her nightgown, and padded barefoot out to the kitchen to put on the coffee.

To Kathy, going barefoot meant springtime. Raised on a farm in Michigan, she had gone barefoot in childhood from the time the first dandelions appeared in the new grass to the time of the first snowfall. Her feet were so tough that she thought sometimes she could walk across a bed of nails without any discomfort.

To Brian, whose own feet were soft and tender as a baby's, the whole idea was upsetting.

"You'll step on something," he told her. "That's the way people get tetanus."

It was one of their minor differences. There were many others. In fact, if a programmer had planned the most unsuitable partnership imaginable, Brian and Kathy Griffin could have been the outcome. Brian had his master's degree in English from Stanford University; Kathy had been a C student in high school and had never gone to college. He had until recently been assistant professor in English at the University of Albuquerque; she had until two months ago worked in the ladies' wear department of a clothing store.

Their personalities were as different as their backgrounds.

"He's a fine man, I'm sure," Kathy's mother had said the first time she met him. "He's certainly brilliant and dedicated to his work. But he's so stiff and serious and—well, truthfully, dear, any man who is still a bachelor at thirty-six has to have *something* the matter with him."

"Perhaps he never met the right woman," Kathy suggested mildly. "Or maybe it just takes him so long to loosen up and break through the ice that all the women he's known have given up and walked off before they ever really got to know him."

"And you've decided to be different? Why?"

"Because I'm stubborn," Kathy had admitted truthfully. "And because I think that Brian Griffin is worth waiting for."

And wait, she did. They had known each other two years before Brian asked her to marry him and another year before that marriage took place.

At the time he proposed, he had told her of his decision to leave the university and take enough education courses to become certified at the high-school level.

"It will be a year before I'll be able to take on the responsibility of a wife," he had told her, "and even then it won't be milk and honey. I'll be making less money than I have been, and there will be a lot less security. I have tenure at the college, which I won't have in high school. I might not even be able to get a job immediately. The country's overstocked with high-school teachers."

"Then why do you want to be one?" Kathy had asked him, puzzled.

"Because there aren't enough *good* ones," Brian had told her. "Many of the kids coming into my classes at the university are all but illiterate. You give them a page to read, and they can't tell you what's on it. Try teaching them the classics, and they can't pronounce the words. Ask them to write about something, and they can't make complete sentences, much less spell anything over two syllables."

"Can't you do anything about it?"

"I try, but it's too late," Brian had said. "By the time they're in college, it's gone too far. They've had twelve years without disciplined learning, and they don't know how to apply themselves. They haven't learned to study or to pace their work so that projects get completed on time. They fall asleep in lectures because they expect to be entertained, not educated.

"We lost a third of our freshman class last year. They dropped out at the end of the first semester."

"And what would you do as a high-school teacher that isn't being done now?"

"I'd *teach*, damn it! I wouldn't baby them or play games with them. I'd push each one into doing the best work of which he or she was capable. By the time they finished a class with me, my college prep students would be able to handle university work."

"And the others?" Kathy had known in her heart that, during her own school years, "the others" would have included her.

"The others would graduate with a knowledge of what disciplined work is all about. That should stand them in good stead, no matter what they decide to do."

"You wouldn't be very popular, I'm afraid."

"I've never been very popular. Anywhere. I have an abrasive personality. Fierce dogs cower when I walk down the street and slink away to hide under porches. Small children run screaming to their mothers. Beautiful girls rip their numbers out of the telephone book and chew them up and swallow them, for fear I might call and invite them out."

"Oh, Brian!" She had burst out laughing. He was so seldom humorous that his awkward attempts at joking touched her deeply.

"And so," he had continued, "Are you willing to wait a year to be the wife of a high-school English teacher? It isn't a very exciting prospect, I must admit. Not nearly as respectable as being the wife of a college professor. I wouldn't blame you—I really wouldn't—"

His sentence had trailed off, unfinished. His eyes had dropped from hers, and she had looked down to see that his hands were clenched in his lap, the knuckles white, the nails making little grooves in his palms. And she had known then how much her answer meant to him.

"Yes," she had said. "I'll wait a year, Bri."

"You're sure it's what you want?"

"I'm sure."

And now, three years later, she was still sure. Kathy had never needed a great deal to make her happy, and what she had now was more than sufficient.

Humming tunelessly beneath her breath, she made the coffee, mixed the frozen orange juice in a pitcher, put bread in the toaster, broke two eggs into a pan.

It was springtime! Under the kitchen window the first hyacinths were blooming. Last week's dust storm was behind them, and the air was fresh and clear and sweet. The nausea that had accompanied her first months of pregnancy was over also. She would eat a good breakfast. Later in the morning she would go out into the yard and sit in a lawn chair in the sunshine.

She glanced up and smiled as Brian came in, his hair slicked down, his hands deftly adjusting the knot in his tie.

"Do all the teachers at Del Norte wear ties to class?"

"No, the riffraff wear open-neck sports shirts."

"Wouldn't that be more comfortable?"

"I like a tie. It gives me dignity." He was only half joking. "I got used to wearing one at the university. Why change now?" He took his seat at the kitchen table and reached for his glass of orange juice. "Call the pharmacy and order a refill on my pills today, will you? I'll pick them up on my way home. That'll be a bit later than usual."

"Oh? A faculty meeting?"

"No, a student wants a conference. I'm meeting her at three. It may take a while. She wants to go over some papers."

"Is she one of your problems?" Kathy asked, sliding the eggs onto a plate and carrying them over to him.

"No, actually she's one of my good ones. Name's Susan McConnell. She's quite a talented writer. Very imaginative. I had them all write final songs for Ophelia. Hers was exceptionally good."

"Have you told her that?"

"Of course not. I don't want her resting on her laurels, thinking she's a genius. She still has things to learn. She tends to get overdramatic. And she's sloppy about details, spelling and punctuation and such. She's not a perfectionist."

"She's still young, Bri." Kathy seated herself across from him. She took a slice of toast and began to spread it with jam. "Most kids are sloppy."

"I'm afraid you're right about that."

"Your own may be. Have you ever thought about that?"

"Brian Junior? Surely, you jest!" His eyes moved fondly to the bulge in the front of her robe. "How is he this morning?"

"Fine and active." She took a bite of toast. "Seriously, Bri, I worry sometimes about that. About your wanting him perfect, and his not measuring up. He might be born with crossed eyes or a birthmark or a harelip or something. Would you still love him?"

"Of course." He was answering her seriously. "He wouldn't be able to help those things. We'd ride with it, take care of him, get him fixed up if we could. He'd still be ours."

"If you really feel that way," Kathy said thoughtfully, "why can't you be more tolerant of your students when *they're* not perfect?"

"Because they can help it. Anybody can look a word up in a dictionary if he doesn't know how to spell it. Time can be planned so that things come in on time. There's no excuse for carelessness.

"The Ruggles boy, for example, came in last week with a real sob story about how he completed his assignment and the wind tore it out of his hands and blew it away. Papers put carefully into a notebook don't blow off. On a windy day, you close a notebook and put it under your arm. That's elementary enough."

"Did he redo the assignment?"

"He did, but I wouldn't accept it. It would set a precedent. If I took one late paper, I'd never be able to refuse the next one. Within a week everything I've taught them about work discipline would be down the drain. The class would be as much of a mess as the one taught by that idiot Luna woman."

"Dolly Luna." She smiled despite herself. "I've got to meet her. After all, the kids dedicated the yearbook to her. Is she really a 'dolly'?"

"Sure is. Two big eyes that open and shut, painted-on smile, head full of sawdust. Ever see a thirty-year-old teenager? That's our Dolly. She doesn't want the kids to think she knows more than they do for fear they won't like her."

Kathy didn't know why, but the metaphor struck her strangely. The grin faded from her lips. She herself smiled a lot. She had never thought about that.

"Brian," she said slowly, "am I—do you think of me—as a 'dolly'?"

"Of course not." He was honestly shocked.

"What am I—when you think of me?"

"You? Why, you're my wife."

"Before that, what was I?"

"You were Kathy. You were real—a person. All you've ever been to me is Kathy."

He took a final swallow of coffee, stood up, took the paper napkin and ran it across his teeth. It was a gesture she hated. If people were that concerned about their teeth, they should brush them one extra time in the morning.

At the same time it made him suddenly so human, so vulnerable, that she wanted to hug him. It was terrible to be married to a man whose weaknesses were his virtues.

"Bri," she said, "I want to ask you a favor. About the McConnell girl."

"What?" He looked surprised.

"If she is really as talented as you say, I want you to tell her. There's something, you know, to handing out something positive. So she overwrites; so she's messy. She's imaginative and bright and special. You said so yourself. I want you to tell her."

"My God, Kathy, you don't even know the kid."

"Yes, I do." She stood her ground. "Not personally, maybe, but I know her. What you just said to me— 'you are real—you're a person—you're Kathy'—that matters, Brian. Tell her that. 'You are real—you are Susan—you are a writer.' You don't have any idea how much it matters, to be real."

"I can't say a thing like that."

"Then write it. Put it on her paper."

"Not the test paper. She didn't do well on that quiz. In fact, it's her worst paper so far. I think she's got a boyfriend."

"Then on another paper. On the song for Ophelia."

"You are a bossy wench!" He made a grab for her. "Kiss me, Kate!"

"Not if you talk in Shakespeare." She pulled back, both pleased and offended. "You're not taking me seriously. I meant it, every word about Susan McConnell. You're taking it too far, Bri. You've got to give them something besides criticism."

"I won't tell you how to cook eggs; you don't tell me how to teach a class. Okay?" He was leaving now, and he was suddenly angry.

Her eyes filled with tears. It was ridiculous how often this happened lately. It must have something to do with being pregnant, she thought. Every time she got mad—or sad—or even happy—she cried.

"Okay," she said, trying to keep her voice steady. "Have a good day. I'll phone the pharmacy for you as soon as it opens. I love you. I'll see you tonight."

"Okay—later."

He was out the door, and for one sharp moment she almost ran screaming after him, "Come back!" That suddenly, that quickly, it struck her—I don't want him to go! *He mustn't go!* Without reason, terror shot through her. But she was as frozen as stone, her lips open to shrill the words that would make him stay.

Something is wrong, she thought wildly. Something terrible! He mustn't go!

And as though her thoughts had been strong enough to reach out and touch him, he was back again. He was bending over her, his hand under her chin, raising her face to his.

"Kathy," he said, "I love you."

"I know," she whispered. "I know."

It was strange, like a formal good-bye. But how could it be, when he would be back so soon, in only a matter of hours? After school, after the conference with the McConnell girl, he would be home.

It will be different, she thought, when the baby comes. It will all be different. Once he's a father, he will be able to give love more easily. He'll be able to reach out to all of them then, and touch them.

It will be different—in only months now—when the baby comes.

SIX

At ten past three on Thursday afternoon, Mrs. Irma Ruggles sat in a chair at her bedroom window and watched the woman in the house next door making her bed. She didn't know the woman's name, but she did know that she was slothful. She never got up in the morning before ten o'clock, and the bed lay open and messy until midafternoon.

Mrs. Ruggles, who was herself up each morning by seven so that her daughter-in-law could give her breakfast and fix her hair before leaving for work, was horrified by such laziness.

"It's better to wear out than to rust out," she quoted self-righteously. "The Lord loves willing hands. Early to bed and early to rise makes the days fly."

The bed-making woman could not possibly have heard her because the windows between them were closed, but she did lift her eyes in time to see the old lady's lips moving and the disapproving expression on her face.

The woman left the half-made bed and walked very

deliberately to the window and pulled down the shade.

"Well, of all the rude things!" Mrs. Ruggles exclaimed in an injured voice, but an instant later her hurt was forgotten as she heard the sound of the front door opening and closing.

Her eyes brightened in anticipation.

"Is that you, Davy?"

"Sure, Gram, it's me."

He came swinging into the room, his schoolbooks under one arm, his windbreaker hung over one shoulder. He bent to kiss her, and he smelled of fresh air and sunshine.

She reached up to ruffle his hair.

"Davy, Davy, you look more like your daddy every day."

"Do I, Gram?"

"The spitting image of him at fifteen."

"I'm seventeen," he reminded her.

"Oh, you can't be, dear. That's just not possible."

"Time gets away from us." He dumped the books on the table by the bed. "I've got something for you. A surprise. I'll be back in just a minute."

"A surprise? Why, what in the world—"

A moment later he was back with a bowl in his hands. "Green Jell-O!"

"Why, I thought there was just that yellow stuff."

"I made this special." He grinned at her. His eyes were very bright. He seemed excited, jumpy and nervous, but at the same time happy. "I fixed it this morning before I went to school so it would be jelled for your snack when I got home."

"What a sweet thing, Davy." She reached for it eagerly. "Aren't you going to get something?"

"Nope. I'm not hungry. I'll sit here with you though

while you eat it. Let's watch some television, shall we?"

"I thought you didn't like daytime TV," she said in surprise. "You know it's the game shows."

"That's okay. I want to see somebody win a race-horse." He clicked on the set and began to fiddle with the dials, adjusting the picture. "How is it? Jelled enough?"

"It's just fine," she said, taking another mouthful.

Actually, it wasn't as tasty as usual, but she didn't want to hurt him by saying so when he had gone to so much trouble to please her. That slightly bitter taste was probably only in her imagination, or more likely her taste buds were failing her, which she supposed happened to people when they got older. All the old pleasures diminished. Nothing worked as well as it once had. Or maybe it was just so long since she had had the green Jell-O that she'd forgotten what it was supposed to taste like.

David turned the dial from one channel to another.

"Oh, hey, cool! Here's that newlywed show where they ask them questions about the things they don't like about each other and stuff. That's a favorite of yours, isn't it?"

"Yes," Mrs. Ruggles said. "I do like that one."

She continued eating.

When the bowl was empty David carried it to the kitchen and washed and dried it and put it back on the shelf. He washed the spoon and dried that also.

When he went back to the bedroom his grand-mother was nodding.

"Tired, Gram?"

"Of course not. What should I be tired from? I'm not one of those people who nap in the daytime. You know that, Davy."

He sat with her until she was asleep, and then he got up and went over to stand by her chair. He looked at her closely. She was breathing heavily and slowly. He reached down and lifted one arm and shoved back the sleeve of the blue flowered robe.

The pulse in her wrist was strong and even. He had not overdone it. But it had taken longer than he had expected.

Leaving the old woman asleep to the canned gaiety of the television game show, David left the house and headed at a run back toward the school.

It was Liz Cline's lead when her hostess, who was dummy, went to answer the telephone.

She came back to say, "That's Betsy for you, Liz. She wants you to call back after this hand."

"Is she at home?" Mrs. Cline asked.

"Yes, and from the sound of things there are boys with her."

"That's normal for Bets. She can't date one boy without taking on all his buddies."

She played out the hand, making game, and excused herself. At the hall phone she dialed her home number.

"Hello, dear. It's Mom. Is something the matter?" The voices in the background were loud and unmistakable. "What *is* Jeff yelling about?"

"Nothing, Mom. He and Mark are just horsing around. We're going to play records."

"All right. Fine. What is it you called about?"

"I just wondered if we could have some of the cake," Betsy said. "I didn't want to cut into it if you were saving it for something."

"Of course I'm not saving it. Cake is for eating. But

keep it controlled, will you? I know how those boys eat. Leave something for dinner."

"Okay," Betsy said, and, muffling the receiver, "Jeff, cool it, will you? My mother's on the phone, and I can hardly hear her."

"And keep the racket down," Liz Cline said, "or the neighbors will have fits."

"Will do. See you later. When do you think you'll be home?"

"Oh, sixish or so I imagine. Good-bye, dear."

She replaced the receiver on the hook and returned to the bridge table.

"I don't know why my daughter has to do everything to extremes. Not only does she date the tallest basketball player on the team, she picks the one with the loudest voice. And that odd friend of his, Mark, never opens his mouth when he's around us, but he must be as bad as Jeff when they're alone. I could hear both of them as though they were right here in the room with me."

"Well, at least you know where she is and who she's got with her." Her hostess shook her head despairingly. "Now, with my Cindy—"

At the Cline house, Betsy hung up the phone and clicked off the cassette tape recorder. The background noise stopped. She took the tape out of the machine and went into the bedroom and put it in the top drawer of her bureau under a pile of underwear.

Then she went into the kitchen and cut three thick slices of chocolate cake and put them on plates. She took out three forks. Using each fork in turn, she systematically took a bite from each of the cake slices. Then she smeared the frosting onto the plates.

She scraped most of the cake off the dishes and put

it down the garbage disposal. Scattering crumbs, she placed the plates and forks in the sink.

She went into the den and switched on the stereo, and the first of the stack of records she had selected dropped into place. She turned up the volume.

Then, like David, she left the house and started back to the school grounds. She had farther to go than David, but she did not have to run. She had Jeff's car.

"I'm here," David said. His face was red and his breath was coming in gasps.

"Yeah, I see," Mark said coldly. "You sure took your own sweet time about it."

"I ran all the way," David said. "The pills took longer to work than I thought they would. You can't regulate something like that."

"You could have doubled the dosage."

"I didn't know how strong they were. Too much could have killed her."

"That's crazy," Jeff said. "Betsy's mom swills them down like there's no tomorrow and she's still alive and kicking."

"My gram's different. She's an old lady."

"Shut up, you guys." Mark's eyes were focused on the door of the building. "Get in the backseat, quick, Dave. I think they're coming."

"They? You mean Sue's *with* him? She was supposed to split and go in the other direction."

David opened the back door of the car and scrambled hastily inside. Pulling the door closed, he disappeared behind the back of the front seat.

"I think—yeah, it's both of them. She's with him all right. She's walking him right out here like a good little puppy dog." Mark gave Jeff a nudge. "Get the mask on."

"No way, man," Jeff said. "I'm not going to show myself. He'll know me by my size."

"You don't have to 'show yourself.' Dave's going to get him from behind. But if he does happen to get an accidental glimpse of you, you'd better have something over your face." Mark was pulling the nylon stocking over his own head. "Okay, you know what to do. He'll go around to the driver's side and get in. When he starts to put the key into the ignition, Dave will stand up and shove the bag down over his head. As soon as he does that, you throw open the door on this side and jump in. Try to get his arms pinned to his sides. I'll run around the front of the car and get him from the driver's side."

"What about Sue?"

"What about her? She'd better get the hell out of the way, that's what. Are you ready?"

"As ready as I'll ever be," Jeff muttered.

The stocking over his face made him feel ridiculous. The eyeholes didn't line up properly, and the nylon half blocked the sight of his left eye. He wondered where Betsy was. She was supposed to be here by this time with his car. What if something had gone wrong and her mother hadn't gone to her bridge club after all or Betsy hadn't been able to contact her there? Or, worse still, what if Betsy had had a wreck on the way over? She wasn't a very good driver, and Jeff's car wasn't the easiest in the world to handle.

We shouldn't have let her take it, he thought now, worriedly. But if she hadn't, she would not have been able to get home in time to set things up and return to the school yard.

He could hear their voices now, Susan's high and strained, Mr. Griffin's crisp and businesslike the way it was when he gave class lectures. It was evidently the end of a discussion that had been started back in the school building.

"—didn't think it would have to be perfect—" Susan was saying, and Mr. Griffin—"That's the whole point, Miss McConnell. Anything worth doing is worth striving to perfect. If you are able to do it well, why should you do it halfway?"

They were beside the car now, on the side facing the building. On the other side Jeff and Mark crouched, heads low, hands braced on knees, in the position of runners waiting for the shot.

"Thank you," Susan said, "for staying to talk with me."

"It's pleasant to have a student show enough interest to request a conference," Mr. Griffin said. He opened the car door and then, unbelievably, asked, "Have you far to go? I have to make a brief stop at a drugstore, but I'll be going straight home from there. I can drop you off at your house on the way."

"Oh, no—no, sir—thank you anyway." Susan's voice was shrill and splintery, anything but normal.

That idiot, Jeff thought angrily. In another minute she's going to be bawling. He's got to suspect something. He'll look in the backseat for sure and see Dave there.

But, no—he was climbing into the car. He was closing the door. Now he was rolling down the window and making some final remark to Susan.

Crouched silent, tense with expectation, Jeff could hear the jangle of the keys. Then there was a thump and Griffin's voice raised sharply in a muffled shout.

"He's got him!" Mark exulted, and then they were both moving.

Jeff had the car door open in an instant and had hurled himself upon the thrashing figure. From his position in the backseat, David was holding the bag down with difficulty as the man in front twisted and shoved at it with frantic hands. Jeff grabbed for his wrists and struggled to bring the arms down to the sides, finding it far less easy than he had anticipated.

A line of poetry sprang into his head, unexpectedly. "Who would have thought the old man had so much strength in him!" No—that wasnt it—it was "blood"— "had so much blood in him." Where had he heard that? In class, of course. It was something from Shakespeare. The realization filled him with a surge of unreasonable fury. That guy Griffin had them brainwashed! Shakespeare was coming out of their ears!

Mark had the other door open now and was trying to loop the rope.

"Pin his arms, damn it!" he growled.

"I'm trying!" Jeff got a grip on Griffin's wrists and heaved himself up so that his entire weight was bearing down on the struggling figure.

"There—that does it! Get the rope around him!"

"Damned bastard's a wildcat!"

"Man, you can say that again!"

Between them they hauled him forward on the seat and began winding the ropes around him as though he were a mummy. Mr. Griffin's efforts were weaker now; they came in spasmlike jerks. He raised his knees suddenly, jabbing Mark in the ribs. Mark brought the flat edge of his hand down hard on the kneecap, and the legs went limp.

"Okay now. I think we've got him where we want him. Let me get this knotted."

"What about the bag?" David panted. "He can't get much air in there. We don't want him to suffocate."

"We've got to leave it on for now," Mark whispered.

"It keeps him quiet, and we don't want him yelling. When we get outside the city limits we'll substitute a blindfold."

"Do you think he can hear with that over his head?"

"Not much, but it's still better to disguise our voices. Don't use names or say anything you don't want him remembering later." Mark's face was glowing. "Hey, boy, didn't I tell you we could do it? It went just perfect!"

"So far, at least." Jeff leaned against the back of the seat, breathing hard. He still found himself astonished at the teacher's strength. "He's a live one, you've got to say that for him. What'll we do now?"

"Just what we planned to do. Take him up to the waterfall."

"But my car isn't here yet."

"We'll take his. The girls can follow when the other car shows up. They know where to go."

From his place in the backseat of the car, David rolled down the window and leaned out. Susan was standing several feet away. Her face was white, and tears were streaming down it.

"What's the matter?" David asked her.

"It was awful—just awful. You said you weren't going to hurt him."

"We didn't. He's fine and dandy. If I pull off this bag, the first thing he'd do would be to spit in my face."

"You said yourself that he can't breathe!"

"If he passes out, we'll open it up. I'll keep watch on that, don't worry. That's my job. I'm 'bag boy.' "

"We're going to go on now," Mark said. "It's too risky to stay parked here. Besides, we don't have too much time if we want our alibis to work for us. You"—he gestured to Susan—"stay here and wait for—*her*. It's best we don't use people's names when we talk about them. As soon as *she* gets here, follow us up. Got it?"

Wordlessly, Susan nodded. The tears kept coming.

"Oh, Christ." Mark shot her a glance of disgust. "Cut the waterworks. Nothing's happened that wasn't supposed to happen. Do you know what you're supposed to do?"

"Yes," Susan whispered.

"Okay. We'll see you there."

Mark turned the key in the ignition and started the engine. It died on him, and he cursed and tried it again. This time it caught, and he pressed down on the accelerator. The car moved slowly across the parking lot and pulled out onto the street.

Standing alone in the empty lot, Susan watched it until it reached the corner. Then it turned east in the direction of the mountains, and she could see it no longer.

It was less than five minutes before Jeff's Ford pulled into the lot with Betsy behind the wheel. When she saw Susan her eyes widened with alarm.

"What happened? Where is everybody?"

"They went on," Susan told her. "They said to tell you to meet them up where we had the picnic."

"Did it work? Did everything go all right? Do they have him tied up and everything?"

"It went—just like it was supposed to," Susan told her.

"And I had to miss all the excitement!" Betsy brought her fist down hard on the edge of the steering wheel. "Everything went fine at my end, and then on the way over here I got stopped by a pig cop. He said I was speeding, which I wasn't. And, of course, I had to explain it was my boyfriend's car, which was why the registration was in his name, not mine. It took forever." She glanced at her watch. "Well, hurry up and get in."

Susan said, "You go without me."

"Why?" Betsy asked. She looked more closely at Susan's face. "Have you been crying? Did something go wrong that you haven't told me about?"

"No, nothing went wrong." Susan bit at her lower lip to stop the trembling. "I just don't want to go, that's all. I've done my part—what I said I'd do. Now I don't want to do anything more."

"But this is the part we've been waiting for! This is when we're really going to bring him down!" Betsy's blue eyes were shining. She had the same bright, sparkling look that she had on the edge of the football field when she was leading a cheer for the winning team. "My gosh, Sue, you don't want to miss out on *this!*"

"I said, I'm not going."

"Well, that's your choice, I guess." Betsy gunned the engine. "Honestly, I don't understand you."

"I don't either, really."

As Mark had said, it had all gone perfectly, just as they had visualized it. But one thing had happened for which she had not been prepared. The word Mr. Griffin had shouted as the bag came down upon him had been, "Run!"

His concern in that instant had not been for himself, but for her.

SEVEN

It was not until she had bypassed the turnoff point by over three miles that Betsy realized that she had come too far, and it took her a long, slow trip back before she was able to locate the dirt road that led to the path by the waterfall. Once she did find it she drove slowly, afraid that a wheel might overrun the trail on one side or the other and sink irrevocably into the soft earth.

Betsy's driving experience was primarily limited to the use of her mother's Volkswagen which could be maneuvered without difficulty on any ground. The width of Jeff's car was intimidating, and the traffic citation she had received earlier in the afternoon had unnerved her.

The experience had been awful. The policeman, whom she had hoped to charm into letting her off with a warning, had not been susceptible. Not only had he been cold and unsympathetic, he had actually seemed grimly pleased to be writing her a ticket.

"You may know my father," she had told him. "Harold Cline. He's on the County Commission."

"I don't know any bigwigs, kid," the policeman had said, "and I'm just as glad. It makes doing my job easier. Either get this paid within five days or make an appointment to appear in court."

He had left her seething, and arriving at the school parking lot to find the preliminary action over had added fuel to the flame of her resentment.

Screw it! They might have waited, she thought angrily. They knew I was coming. They could have stalled somehow till I got there.

Betsy was not accustomed to being thwarted. For most of her life she had gotten what she wanted when she wanted it. An only child, she had been born conveniently to parents who wanted a daughter. The fact that she had also been born blond and cuddly and had smiled early and often had made her reception even warmer.

By the time she was a year old, Betsy had accepted the fact that little girls who handed out smiles and kisses could name their own rewards, and the self-confidence this knowledge gave her served her well. In kindergarten she was selected to serve the juice and hand out pencils; in grammar school she collected more Valentines and received more phone calls than anyone in her class. To be "Betsy Cline's good friend" was an honor eagerly sought by her classmates, and to be "somebody Betsy doesn't care for" was social suicide. When Shauna Bearman, a black-haired, porcelain complexioned beauty, was selected to play Snow White in the fifth-grade play, she found herself the only one in the class excluded from Betsy's tenth birthday party, and was thereafter totally ostracized. Peer pressure reached such a point that on the night of the play Shauna burst into tears on stage and the curtain had to be lowered. In the Christmas Nativity Tableau,

Betsy Cline was Mary, and her teacher sighed with relief.

"Thank the Lord we've got one little actress without temperament," she told everyone.

Betsy was being asked for dates by the time she was
eleven, and once in high school she was the only freshman to attend the senior prom. Adults considered her
unspoiled and wholesome. Her contemporaries liked
her for her sparkle and charm. The fact that she was
not traditionally pretty helped her popularity, for it
kept boys from being uncomfortable around her and
girls from being jealous.

"Cute" was the word people used for her, and it was
the way she thought of herself.

"I'd rather be cute than beautiful," she had said
once to her mother, who had smiled and agreed.

"It lasts longer," Mrs. Cline had told her. "Pretti-
ness fades, but a girl can be cute right into middle
age."

There were only two people she knew who seemed
immune to Betsy's cuteness, and one was Mr. Griffin.
This semester, for the first time in her life, she had
found her papers getting marked down for such things
as "lack of originality" and "overuse of clichés."

"I don't know what he means," she had complained
to her parents, who were as bewildered as she. "What's
wrong with saying things the way other people have if
it's the best way to say them? You can't just make
words up out of the air."

Her mother had written Mr. Griffin a note request-
ing that he "go easier on Betsy, who is very sensitive to
criticism," and her father had offered to go to the
principal and have her moved to another section of
senior English.

Betsy had left the note in Mr. Griffin's box in the

office. She found it later, returned with one of her papers, with a notation on the bottom that said, "The best way to avoid criticism is not to earn it." The paper had received a D.

She had turned down her father's offer, saying, "It just isn't right to change classes. If one person does it, then everybody will want to." The truth was that she would not have left the class for anything in the world. It was the only class all day that she had with Mark Kinney.

Mark was the other person in Betsy's life who did not seem to notice her cuteness. At first she had thought it was because of Lana. There were boys who were attracted only to older women, and Lana, a college sophomore, had had a certain sophistication about her that Betsy could never equal. But after the thing had happened last semester, when Mr. Griffin had recognized Mark's term paper as one he had read several years before when he was teaching at the University of Albuquerque and had carried the thing to such extremes—dropping Mark from the class, checking with the college English Department to determine who had access to the file of past papers—Lana's father had had her transferred to a small college in the southern part of the state.

"I want her out from under that boy's influence," he had been heard to say. "He'a sick kid. My daughter would never have thought of rifling that file if he hadn't put her up to it. She's obsessed by him. If he told her to jump out a window, she'd do it. It's gone far enough, and I want her out of here, now."

So Lana was out of the picture, and Betsy was secretly overjoyed. Surely now Mark would notice her as someone more than just a girl who dated his best friend. But it did not seem to happen. Nor did Mark appear to grieve particularly over the loss of Lana. He remained the same as he had always been—cool, expressionless, in complete control of every situation—except the one in which he had been forced by Mr. Griffin to plead for reentry to the class. He accepted Betsy, as he always had, as part of a group of which he himself was the center. But he made no effort to see her alone or to advance their relationship any further.

Well, she was worth noticing, and today, Betsy thought, she had proved it. It was she who had provided the alibis for them all.

"We'll use my cassette recorder," she had told them, "and we'll be able to plant voices anywhere we want them." She had even thought through to the disposal of the cake.

"No originality, huh?" she had remarked to herself with satisfaction. "This should be original enough for anybody."

And it had gone almost perfectly. When her mother got home from her bridge club, three dirty plates in the sink would testify to the fact that three hungry teenagers had spent the afternoon there. She had left the house in Jeff's car in plenty of time to make the action at the school ground. She even had her own nylon stocking mask in her purse. It was the stupid policeman who had fouled up everything by stopping her when she was barely enough over the speed limit to register on the speedometer.

The more she thought about it the angrier she became, and by the time she reached the clearing where Mark had parked Mr. Griffin's dull green Chevrolet her initial enthusiasm was masked by fury.

She ran the car up to a point where it paralleled Mr. Griffin's, gave the key a twist, and got out. The entrance to the path, widened by the unusual amount of traffic, was no longer completely concealed by the rock. Quickly Betsy shoved aside the few interfering branches and began the short hike that would take her back to the waterfall.

The condition of the path showed that Mr. Griffin had not been led along it without a struggle. The earth was scuffed and in places bushes were trampled and broken. At one spot there had evidently been a major scuffle, for there was an imprint in the soft earth as though someone had fallen heavily, and on the ground were some scattered coins that had apparently tumbled from a pocket. A few feet farther there lay a plastic vial containing several pills. Betsy picked the vial up, noting that the name on the label was "Brian Griffin."

She hastened her footsteps, and suddenly she was upon them. Pulling herself to a halt, she drew in her breath with a combination of shock and delight. There on the ground before her, tied and blindfolded, lay Mr. Griffin. The startling part was that he did not look much different than he did in the classroom. The blindfold across his eyes only slightly diminished the severity of the sharp nose, the neat mustache, the straight, firm mouth. His shirt and jacket were smeared with dirt, but the neatly knotted tie was perfectly in place.

Betsy's mood of anger fell away as though it had never existed.

"It's just like he was getting ready to give a lecture!" she breathed in amazement.

Jeff motioned her to silence. Coming over to stand beside her, he said in a low voice, "You can't talk out like that. You've got to put on an accent or talk through your nose or something. We don't want him to recognize our voices, remember?" He glanced behind her. "Where's Sue?"

"She wouldn't come."

"Why not?"

"I don't know. She just didn't want to. She looked like she'd been crying."

"That's all we need, to have that broad crack up on us." Jeff put an arm around her shoulders. "I'm glad you're a chick with guts. This guy Griffin's a scrapper. He's not the pushover we thought he'd be. We may have to rough him up a little to get him where we want him."

"I wouldn't miss this for the world," Betsy said excitedly. She found her breath coming faster as she and Jeff moved closer to the man on the ground, standing so that they could stare down into his face.

Mark and David were on their knees beside him.

"So how does it feel?" Mark was asking in a high, nasal twang, as though he had just been imported from the back hills of the Ozarks. "How do you like it being on the ground for a change? It's not so great is it, being down where people can walk on you? Well, now you know how your students feel all the time."

Mr. Griffin lay silent. Only the straining of the tendons in his neck showed that he was conscious and listening.

"Well, how does it feel?" Mark repeated. "We want an answer. Did you hear me—*sir?*"

"Yes, I heard you," Mr. Griffin said shortly.

"Your answer—*sir?*"

"My answer," Mr. Griffin said in his cold, clipped voice, "is that if you know what's good for you, you'll untie this rope this instant. If it's money you're after, I don't have any on me. I carry a checkbook."

"We don't want your money," David said. "We're not thieves."

"What are you then?" Mr. Griffin asked him. "Besides punks and kidnappers, that is?"

"We are your students, present, past and future," Mark told him, the corner of his mouth twitching slightly with the closest Betsy had ever seen him come to a smile. "We are representatives of every poor kid who has ever walked into your dungeon of a classroom. We come to bring you 'the slings and arrows of outrageous fortune.' We're here to deliver revenge."

"If this is a joke," Mr. Griffin said, "it's not funny. It's the sort of childish demonstration I'd expect from five-year-olds, not high-school seniors. How many of you are there?"

"A lot," Jeff said. "Twenty—twenty-five—thirty!" He glanced at Betsy and grinned. "Would you believe fifty—a hundred—everybody who's ever had to take a class from you?"

"That's ridiculous. There can't be more than three of you. I've only heard three voices. And all of you are boys."

Mark glanced up at Betsy and nodded.

"Are you sure of that?" she asked, holding her nose as she spoke so that her voice came out as nasal as Mark's had been. "I'm not a boy. There are a lot of us girls who hate you too, you know."

Mr. Griffin gave a start of surprise. Quite evidently he had not expected this. "Then there was another car," he said. "Some of you came in another car."

"There are lots of other cars," Jeff said. "Dozens of them. I told you, we're all here. None of us wanted to miss this."

"Miss what?"

There was a slight pause. Then Mark said, "Nobody wanted to miss watching you die."

"You want me to believe that you brought me here to kill me? Just because you don't like the way I teach? That's ridiculous."

"You used that word before," David said. "You're repeating yourself. You shouldn't use the same adjective twice in a row like that, you know?"

"You're sick," Mr. Griffin said.

"All of us?"

"All of you who are in on this. I'm sure it can't be the entire class. There can't be that many teenage monsters wandering loose around Del Norte."

"Talking about 'sick,'" Betsy volunteered suddenly, "look what I found!" She held up the vial.

The boys turned to look at her.

"What is it?" Jeff asked.

"A container of pills I found back there on the path. It's Mr. Griffin's. It's—" She studied the label— "This can't be right. It says it's 'nitroglycerin.'"

"You mean the explosive?" David broke into laughter. "Maybe he was one jump ahead of us and was planning to blow up the school."

"'Take one for pain of angina,'" Betsy continued reading. "What's that?"

"Yeah, what's that, Mr. G.?" Mark gave him a hard prod with his balled fist. "Wake up down there. Don't take a nap on us."

"Untie these ropes," Mr. Griffin said icily.

"I guess he doesn't want to answer." Jeff took the vial out of Betsy's hand, opened it, and poured a few pills into the palm of his own hand. "Is this stuff really nitroglycerin? Will it blow up?"

There was no response from the man on the ground.

"Let's try it and see." Bending down, he placed the

pills in a small pile on the top of a flat rock. He picked up another, smaller rock and held it poised over them. "How high will it blow, Mr. G.? Is this gonna shake the forest?"

"It won't detonate," Mr. Griffin said. "There's not enough explosive in those to amount to anything. They're for medical use only."

"They won't explode, huh? Well, we'll see about that. Stand back, everybody." Jeff brought the stone down hard and the pills crumbled into powder. "Well, hey, now, he was telling the truth. Nothing happened."

"Put those back in my pocket," Mr. Griffin said.

"He can't. They're gone." David was leaning over him, reaching to check the rope around his wrists. He paused and then asked in his natural voice, "What's that ring?"

"My wedding band."

"No, the other ring. The one with the tree on it. I've seen that before someplace."

"Watch your voice," Mark hissed.

"What's the ring with the tree?" David struggled to force his voice into an accent that was a mixture of French and Spanish, but his eyes did not move from Mr. Griffin's right hand. "Have you always worn that ring?"

"It's my college ring. Yes, I've always worn it. How long are you going to keep playing this game? Take off the blindfold. I want to see who you are."

"How about begging us, Mr. Griffin?" Mark said quietly.

"*Begging* you? To take off the blindfold?"

"We want to hear you beg." Mark's eyes were shining dark pockets under the half-lowered lids. "To take off the blindfold, sure. To untie you, sure. But isn't

there something more worth begging for? Like your
life?"

"You really want me to believe you're planning to
commit murder?"

"You'd better believe it, because it's true."

"Why? What would you gain by doing an insane
thing like that?"

"I told you before—revenge. Revenge for every
stingy, cruel, rotten, stinking thing you've ever done to
us, any of us. You made *us* crawl—now, you shit, we're
going to make *you* crawl. Beg us, Mr. G.! Plead with
us! Let's hear you whine!"

"I most certainly will not," Mr. Griffin said.

"God, he's a stubborn bastard," Jeff said under his
breath to Betsy. "You've almost got to like him a little,
you know?"

"*I* don't like him." She moved closer and bent over,
studying the man's face. She had never been this close
to Mr. Griffin before. She could see the afternoon
growth of hair prickling beneath the smooth white
skin and the black mustache moving slightly with the
breath from his nostrils. His neck was thin and pale
and his Adam's apple jutted out like a doorknob. She
thought, he's ugly. Even uglier than the policeman. In
her mind the two images drew together, overlapped,
and became one. If she were to remove the blindfold,
she knew she would find beneath it the policeman's
cold, insolent stare.

"Make him cry," she said to Mark. "I want to see
him cry."

"He'll cry, all right. We'll make him cry if it takes a
week." Mark's face was flushed and feverish looking.
"How about a nice, slow death, Mr. G.? Like lying
right here on the ground and starving to death?"

"I don't believe you would do that. You have too much to lose."

"We don't have anything at all to lose. All we have to do is go home and leave you here. Nobody will ever find you. Nobody knows about this place but us."

The man on the ground made no answer.

"Look," Jeff said, aside to Mark, "time's running out on us. We need to get back if the things we've set up are going to work. Maybe we ought to loosen the ropes so he can work his way out of them and take off. What do you think?"

"I think you're nuts," Mark said. "He doesn't get out of here till he begs. We agreed on that."

"But it doesn't look like he's going to."

"He's going to. Don't you worry your head about that. He'll break."

"But we're out of time."

"Then we'll leave him," Mark said.

"Leave him? You mean right here?"

"It's as good a place as any."

Mark got to his feet. "Do you hear that, Mr. G.? You're in for a long, cold night. Want to change your mind?"

"Absolutely not."

"Your wife will worry about you."

"I'm sure she will. She'll also call the police."

"A lot of good that will do her. They'll never look for you here, you can be sure of that." Mark dropped his hand to David's shoulder. "Hey, what's with you? Wake up, boy."

"I'm with you." David got up slowly. "Look, let's have a talk."

"What about? There's nothing to talk over."

"Yes, there is. Come down this way." He drew Mark

a few yards downstream and dropped his voice. "We can't do that. It's carrying the game too far. Why don't we take him back now, the way we planned? He won't forget today, that's for sure. We've scared him plenty. That's what we were after, wasn't it?"

"He hasn't begged yet. He's got to *beg*."

"That really doesn't matter, does it? I mean, just saying the words?"

"It matters to *me*." Mark's voice was like a gray steel knife. "He made *me* beg, remember? 'Please, Mr. G., let me back into your class. I'll be a good boy. I won't cheat again.' And then he wouldn't do it. 'Next semester,' he said. 'Next semester you can take it over again.' He had me where he wanted me, didn't he? No English credit, no graduation. And the principal backed him up. No other English class would do. It was Griffin's or nothing. Remember?"

"I remember. But, my God, Mark—"

"He's going to beg. And he's going to stay here until he does."

Jeff and Betsy had moved to join them, catching the end of his statement.

"But what if he never does?" Jeff asked. "He's got more backbone than we bargained for. We can't just leave him here till he starves."

"He'll break before then." Beneath the heavy lids, Mark's eyes were glistening. "Look, if we let him go now, he's *won*."

"Mark's right," Betsy said. "He thinks he's really something. He called us 'five-year-olds.' He thinks we're 'ridiculous.' "

"But how long can we keep him here?"

"Long enough to crack him. Man, he'll break," Mark said determinedly. "I promise you that. He'll break, and he'll beg, and he'll crawl, just the way we planned, and when he gets back in that classroom he'll be a shell, man, just a shell. He'll look out at that class, and he'll know somewhere out there, scattered around behind those Shakespeare books, there are a bunch of kids who watched him crawl. He'll know they're picturing him here on the ground, begging. Don't you think that's going to do something to him?"

"Don't go soft, Jeff," Betsy said. "You're the one who was talking about having 'guts.'"

"I'm not going soft," Jeff said defensively. "It's Dave who said we should take him back."

"Well—I still don't like it," David said. "If we do leave him awhile, we'll have to come back up here later. It can't be all night."

"I've got a game tonight," Jeff said. "And Betsy's got to cheer. We can come back up after that."

"It'll be like midnight!"

"So?" Mark said. "That'll give him plenty of time to think things over—to wonder if we're ever coming. Are you with me?"

"Of course," Betsy said.

"It's not so long," Jeff said. "Like, till midnight isn't that long. Maybe seven hours."

"Dave?"

"I guess I don't have a choice, do I?" David said. "I'm outvoted."

"Damned right you are." Mark turned on his heel and walked back upstream to where Mr. Griffin lay, unmoving, by the waterfall. "Goodnight, Mr. G. Enjoy your own company. It's all you're going to have for a long time. Here's your last chance. Going to ask us, 'pretty please' to let you go?"

The man on the ground did not answer.

"To hell with you, then—*sir*," Mark said. "Come on, you guys."

He led the way, and the others fell into step behind him.

Betsy turned to throw one last look at the man by the stream. He was lying very still. Only his chest was moving—up and down—up and down—as though he had been running hard.

Betsy had a sudden childish impulse to run back and step on his face.

EIGHT

The first time David phoned, Mr. McConnell answered.

"I'm sorry," he said. "Sue's lying down. She doesn't feel too well tonight."

The second time he called, an hour later, he received the same answer, this time from a brother.

At this point he asked his mother, "Can I use the car for a while tonight?"

"Why?" she asked, surprised.

There was no reason not to be truthful.

"There's a girl I'd like to talk to."

"Oh?" his mother said with interest. "The same girl you took to the picnic last weekend?"

"That's the one."

"I think it's nice," Mrs. Ruggles said, "that you're interested in a girl. What's she like, Davy? Why haven't you told me about her?"

"I did. I said I was taking her to the picnic."

"I know, but you made it sound like she was just

one of a group. Tonight you want to see her alone. That must mean that she's at least a little special."

"She's just a girl," David said. "She's in one of my classes."

"Is she pretty?"

"Not really." That sounded funny. He rephrased it. "You might not think so. She's very bright."

"I've wondered what sort of girl you would be attracted to. Your father liked them pretty."

"I guess he must have," David said dutifully. "He married you, didn't he?"

"No, I mean later. He liked them very pretty and innocent and young. Of course, he looked so young himself. I'm sure they never guessed he was the father of a child. Do you remember him at all, Davy—your father?"

"Yes," David said, going tense inside as he always did when they touched upon this subject. "He used to play on the floor with me and pretend he was a bear."

"Yes, he was perfectly happy to romp with you. He was playful, like a little boy himself. It was the responsibility of supporting and raising you that he couldn't face up to." His mother's expression was strange, torn, half wanting to remember, half closing the door upon everything. The closed door won. "What's your girl friend's name?"

"She's not a girl friend. Just a regular friend. Her name's Sue."

"A nice, down-to-earth name. All right, take the car, but for heaven's sake, drive carefully. When will you be home?"

"Not late, Mom."

"Be sure you're not. I won't be able to sleep until you're home, and I have to work in the morning."

And then, unpredictably, she smiled and asked, "Do you need some money?"

"No, thanks. I have a little. Besides, we won't be doing anything much."

"Have a good time," she said. And she handed him the keys.

When he reached Susan's house and rang the doorbell, Mrs. McConnell answered.

"Oh, hello, David." She remembered his name. "Sue isn't feeling well, but I'm sure she'll want to see *you*. Sit down and I'll go check on her and see if she's awake."

A few moments later she came back downstairs, and her daughter was with her.

"Hello, David," Susan said stiffly. Her eyes shifted past his, not quite meeting them. She did, indeed, look sick. Her nose was red and her face was puffy and bruised looking.

"I've got the use of the car tonight," he told her. "I thought you might want to take a ride somewhere and maybe get something to eat."

"Why don't you, dear?" Mrs. McConnell said. "You hardly ate any dinner. Go get a sandwich or something, and then come back and get a good night's sleep."

"Okay," Susan said. He could see that she did not want to go but was afraid not to. The thing that had happened that afternoon could not be shoved away.

They went out to the car, and he opened the door for her. Then he went around to the driver's side and got in. He pulled the door closed, and they sat a moment in silence.

Finally, David said, "The Snack-'n-Soda all right?"

"Anyplace. I'm not hungry." Her voice was ragged.

"I couldn't swallow food right now if you paid me to. What did you do to him, Dave, after you left the school?"

"Just what we said we were going to do. We took him up to the place by the waterfall, and Mark tried to scare him. It didn't work very well. I mean, he didn't scare as easily as Mark had thought he would. Mark had to keep talking to him."

"Was the bag still over his head?"

"No, of course not. We took that off as soon as we got out of the city. He's blindfolded."

"He *is* blindfolded?" Susan regarded him incredulously. "Do you mean he's *still* blindfolded? You didn't let him go?"

"Not yet," David said. "I thought we should, but the others outvoted me. They want to keep him tied up till he breaks. Mark wants to hear him beg to be let go."

"Where is he? What have you done with him?"

David turned the key and started the engine.

"You may not want to eat," he said, "but we can't just sit here in front of your house. Your folks will wonder what's the matter. Let's just drive around for a while."

"I asked you, where is he?"

"Up in the mountains at the picnic place, like I told you."

"You *left* him there!" Susan exclaimed in horror.

"Don't sound so tragic," David said defensively. "Nothing's going to hurt him. Mark and Jeff are going back up there tonight after Jeff's game's over. Griffin will have thought things over by then. He'll say what Mark wants him to. Then they'll bring him down and turn him loose like we planned.

"Don't worry, Sue. He'll be in class tomorrow, you'll

see. He'll be shook up a little, maybe, but he'll be there."

"I couldn't face him if he were," Susan said. "I'd start to cry if I even looked at him. He thought—" Her voice broke. "He thought *I* was the one in danger. Did you hear him when you grabbed him? He called out, 'Run!' He wanted me to get away."

"You heard him wrong."

"David, I didn't!" Susan insisted. "He cared about me—he wanted to save me! We can't just leave him up there alone in the dark. It's too dreadful! We've got to go get him!"

"I told you, Mark and Jeff are going to do that. It won't be long now."

"How can you know that? Those games run till after eleven. By the time Jeff gets showered and changed and out of there it could be midnight. Then, who knows—maybe they'll decide not to go at all. Maybe they'll tell each other, 'We'll do it in the morning.' "

"They wouldn't do that," David said, but even as he spoke a shadow of a doubt shifted across his mind. Was it possible that they might do exactly what Susan was suggesting? As she said, it would be late, and Jeff would be tired and hungry. He never ate before a game and was always starving afterward. It was not inconceivable that he and Betsy and Mark might stop somewhere for a hamburger, and time would slip by. It would be Betsy's curfew. Jeff would have to take her home, and then there would be just himself and Mark. Jeff was the one who owned the car, and if he was worn out from the game—

"They wouldn't do that," David said again, but his uncertainty showed in his voice. "At least, I don't think they would."

"We can't take the chance," Susan said. "We've got to go up there right now."

"Up to the mountains? Are you kidding? Just you and I—without Mark?"

"We can untie him and bring him down as well as they can. It's gone too far, Dave. It isn't fun anymore. When you told me about it at first—at the picnic—I thought it would be—fun. But it isn't. It's—it's awful."

She was crying now. In the faint light from the streetlamp at the corner, David could see the glitter of her tears sliding out from under the rim of her glasses and making shiny streaks down the sides of her face. The sight upset him more than he would have expected.

"Well," he said, "hell—I guess we could. It's just that Mark would be so pissed off. When he plans something he likes it to go his way."

"Why should what Mark wants matter so much? We're in this just as much as he is, aren't we? Why shouldn't what *we* want matter?"

"You don't understand," David told her. "Mark isn't like other people. He's—he's—" He struggled to find the words he wanted and was unable to do so. Mark was Mark. It was that simple. You didn't try to explain Mark, you just accepted him.

"But Mark's not here now, and we are. Please, David, we've got to go up there! We can't leave him a minute longer!" Her words came out in a strangled sob, and David felt his heart twist suddenly within him.

"Okay," he said gruffly. "Okay, you win. Just stop the sniffling, will you?"

He threw the car into gear and stepped on the accelerator.

They didn't talk much during the drive to the mountains. David, whose experience in night driving was almost nonexistent, kept his eyes focused on the limited strip of road that lay exposed in the path of the headlights. He was acutely conscious of the girl on the seat beside him. She was sitting very straight and still with her hands gripped together in her lap. Her head was bent, and her hair fell forward so that when he glanced sideways he could not see her face.

At one point he asked, "Are you still crying?"

"No. Not anymore."

"Do you want to move over this way?"

Wordlessly she slid over on the seat so that she was close beside him, her shoulder touching his. She reached up and took off her glasses and wiped the lenses on the front of her blouse.

"I didn't mean to make such a fuss," she said in a small voice. "It's just—the thought of him up there alone—"

"I know. It's okay."

To his surprise, he found he really meant it. At the moment he felt calmer—better—happier than he had for a long time. The car interior was a world in itself. He and this girl, whom he had hardly known before the past week, were its only inhabitants. Outside the car windows darkness poured past them and drew together behind them, blocking out further reality.

With his hands upon the steering wheel and the gas pedal under his foot, David knew a strange, exhilarating sense of freedom. His mother, his grandmother, school, sinks full of dishes, bowls of lime-colored gelatin, were left far behind him. What would it be like, he wondered, to keep on driving, to never come back? What if he didn't turn north onto the road into the mountains but stayed instead on the highway, following it as far as it went, all the way to the coast? He tried to imagine what it would be like there, the air moist and salty, waves pounding upon sparkling beaches, gulls circling and screaming overhead.

"Did you ever see the ocean?" he asked Susan.

"Yes," she said, surprised at the question. "Two summers ago my folks took us to California."

"Was it nice?"

"We had a pretty good time. The beaches were fun. Then Mel, my little brother, cut his foot on some barnacles and had to go to the emergency room for stitches. Things like that always happen on our vacations."

"I've never been to either coast," David said. "I was just thinking what it would be like if we kept on driving until we reached the water."

"Then we could take a ship," Susan said, "and go on farther and find an uninhabited island. People back here would think we'd disappeared off the face of the earth."

"You think about things like that too?"

"Someday I'm going to live completely alone in a cabin a million miles from anywhere and think and read and write poetry and maybe even novels." She paused and then asked tentatively, "Do you think that's crazy, wanting to do that?"

"That's not crazy," David said. "My father—" He stopped himself.

"Yes?"

"He did something like that, I think. Just left and went and did his thing, without worrying about what people thought. He looked like me. My gram says he did, anyway, and there's a picture of him I found, and I remember a little. I remember his hands. They were thin and strong and they were always gentle when they touched me. Did you ever notice Griffin's hands?"

"No," Susan said. "Not really. Should I have?"

"I guess there's no reason you would. I never noticed them myself until this afternoon when we were tying him up, and all of a sudden I got this funny feeling. There was something about his hands that reminded me of my father."

"How odd," Susan said. "Shouldn't the turnoff be right along here someplace?"

"I think so. It's hard to tell at night." David squinted into the darkness. "Is that it—that road there? That *is* a road, isn't it? Yes, I think that's it."

"Let's try it," Susan said. "If we're wrong it just means backing out and starting over."

David turned the car onto the dirt trail and inched it forward, the headlights throwing back strange shapes and shadows as trees and bushes and rocks emerged from the depths of the darkness and crept past them and fell away again as new forms took their places.

"It's the right road," he said.

"How can you tell?"

"I remember how it took a jog to the right. You can't see it now, but there's a big, craggy sort of rock there on the left."

"I can't see *anything*," Susan told him. "Just what's directly ahead of us." Some time later she asked, "Haven't we come too far?"

"No way. We go to the end, remember?"

"But it's taking so long."

"That's because I'm driving so slowly. All we need is to get stuck here. That would really fix things."

They drove on in silence, and then, suddenly, they were at the clearing.

Susan caught her breath with a little gasp. "Someone's here!"

"No. That's Griffin's car."

"You left it parked right here where anybody could see it?"

"Who's going to see it? Nobody comes up this far, especially at night." He pulled up next to the Chevrolet and turned off the ignition and the headlights. Immediately they were overwhelmed by silence. Complete. Unbroken. Heavy. Weighted. The absolute stillness of a forest at night.

For a long moment they sat, unmoving. When Susan spoke at last it was in a whisper.

"It's so—black."

"There's a flashlight in the glove compartment. My mother keeps it there in case of emergencies." David reached across her and groped along the dashboard. He located the button and pressed it, and the front of the glove compartment swung down and he reached inside. For one awful moment he thought the light was not there, but then he found it, shoved back under some papers. He took it out and pushed the door back into place.

"Okay," he said. "Are you ready?"

Without waiting for her answer, he pulled the handle and opened the car door. He got out, and his feet crunched loudly into dried leaves and dead branches.

"Wait," Susan said, "I'll come out your side," and she slid out behind him.

For some inexplicable reason, David could not bring himself to slam the car door. The sound would have cut through the stillness like a gunshot. Instead, he let it ease into place, and then he pressed the switch to turn on the flashlight. The thin beam shot ahead of them, illuminating the path entrance.

"Okay?" he asked.

"Okay," Susan said shakily. And then—"Dave, think how dark—how terribly dark it must be—back where he is! Think how it must be for him lying there, all alone, not knowing if anybody's going to come—ever!"

"Well, we're here now, so he doesn't have to lie there much longer," David said reassuringly.

He took her hand. It felt small and cold in his, and he squeezed it hard. There was no reason for a girl like Susan to be here, frightened and remorseful, staggering around the mountain darkness. Why had he drawn her into this crazy plot? he asked himself angrily. Why, indeed, had he been drawn into it himself? It had been a dumb idea right from the beginning. People didn't go around kidnapping other people just because they didn't like them. There was nothing amusing about it, nothing to be gained by doing it. If anyone but Mark had suggested it, he would have told him he was nuts. But somehow with Mark things always seemed so sensible. When Mark looked at you with those odd, gray eyes of his, when Mark spoke your name and put his hand on your shoulder—

"How long has it been since you did something crazy, just for the hell of it?" Mark had asked him, and it had been as though he had reached straight into him and placed a finger on the open sore at the core of his soul.

After that things had happened so fast there had been no time for reconsidering. It had all been there before them, laid out the way it should go. He had been swept up by the plan as completely as though it had been his own. He had thought of calling Susan—or had he? Was it he or someone else who had suggested that? He had hardly known Susan at that point.

To him she had been no more than a studious, shy little mouse of a girl who had tried to help him catch his papers when the wind had caught them.

"Well, let's go," he said. "The sooner we get there, the sooner it's done. He's going to be one mad dude when we get to him."

The beam of the flashlight led them forward, and a moment later the bushes had closed in behind them. A few paces more and they could hear the waterfall. It grew louder and louder—much louder than it had seemed in the daytime—as though the whole night was made up of rushing water.

As they approached the stream bank, David tightened his grip on Susan's hand.

"There's no way we're going to get him out of here without untying him," he told her. "You do know that, don't you? If Jeff were here, he could do it. He'd just drag him out with the ropes and blindfold still on him. But I'm not a burly athlete. We'll have to untie him here and let him walk out."

"I know."

"What I mean is, he'll see who we are. There's no way to prevent it. We're really letting ourselves in for it. He can have us expelled."

"I know," Susan said again. "It doesn't matter. I mean, of course, it matters, but we don't have any choice, do we?"

"I guess not," David said.

The light moved ahead and fell upon him—the man by the stream.

He was lying exactly as he had been when they left him, straight and still, the blindfold neatly in place. A cry broke from Susan's lips, and she dropped David's hand and hurried froward.

"Oh," she moaned, dropping to her knees beside the

till figure. "Oh, Mr. Griffin, I'm sorry! I'm so sorry—so sorry—" Her voice broke, and she grasped the rope at the man's wrists, fumbling for the knot. David, I can't find the end! How did you tie this? Oh, please, hurry and get this off him. It's cutting the circulation."

"Here—it goes all the way around behind." David knelt down beside her. "I'm sorry too, sir. This was a dumb, rotten thing to do. We'll have you undone in a minute. Try to roll over sideways so I can reach the knot in back."

The man did not move.

"He's asleep," Susan said in amazement. "How could he be asleep with the ground so hard? Mr. Griffin, wake up! Please, wake up! We're here to take you home!"

"Move back, Sue," David said hoarsely.

"But, we've got to wake him—"

"I said, move back. Let me get at the blindfold." He gripped the cloth with numb fingers and yanked it upward until it slid off the forehead and onto the ground. Then he lifted the flashlight and turned the beam straight into the man's face.

"His eyes are open," Susan breathed. "He's not asleep. His eyes are open!"

"He's not asleep," David agreed softly.

"Then why doesn't he move? Why doesn't he say something? Mr. Griffin, it's Sue—Susan McConnell—from your lit class, remember? Please, Mr. Griffin—"

David turned the light away from the wide, unblinking stare of the man on the ground beside him.

"He's not asleep," he said. "He's dead."

NINE

We've got to get to Mark!

The single sentence screamed again and again through his brain.

We've got to get to Mark! Mark will know what to do.

It got him back down the path, dragging Susan behind him, stumbling, falling once, getting up again, Susan's wrist still tightly encircled by his hand. It got him into the car, the key into the ignition, the engine into life. It took them back along the dirt road without running off the side into the underbrush, onto the highway without swerving and running headlong into an oncoming car.

We've got to get to Mark. Mark will know what to do. He said it aloud, emphasizing each word.

"To *do?* How can anybody do anything?" Susan said. "You can't make a dead person come alive."

She wasn't crying. Susan, whose tears had fallen continuously since the middle of the afternoon, was no longer weeping. David glanced sideways at her there on the seat beside him, dry-eyed and expressionless, her lips pressed tightly together except when they parted to let the thin, flat voice come through.

"There's nothing Mark can do," Susan said. "We're murderers."

"We didn't kill him! We hardly touched him! I swear it, Sue, nobody roughed the guy up. He was fine when we left him. You know what he said to us? Mark told him, 'Beg us, Mr. G. Plead with us,' and he said, 'I most certainly will not.' Does that sound like a guy who's been banged around?"

"People don't just die, for no reason."

"*This* guy did. I swear it—honestly—we didn't hurt him. The worst we did was tie the rope around him. That could never kill anybody." David bore down on the accelerator. "We've got to get to Mark. He'll know how to handle things—who to call—what to do. What the hell do you do when somebody's dead like that, for no reason, way out in the mountains? Who goes and gets them? An ambulance couldn't ever make it up that road."

"We can go to my house and get my dad," Susan said. "He'll help us."

"Mark first. We can't do anything until we tell Mark. My God, Sue, why did we have to be the ones to find him? If you hadn't insisted we go up there it would have been Mark and Jeff. They'd have taken care of things. It was crazy for us to have gone up there without telling them or anything."

They pulled into the Del Norte parking lot. It was seething with activity; voices shouted, headlights blinked on in all directions, car horns blasted as automobiles tried to inch their way into the creeping lines of traffic.

"The game must just be over," Susan said. "You'll never find him in this."

"Sure I will. We're in luck; there are parking spaces." There was one right ahead of him, and David pulled into it, braking and shifting suddenly so as to bypass the fender of the car next to him. "Come on, let's get in there."

"I'm not going."

"What do you mean you're not going?"

"I just can't face it. All those people, yelling and screaming because we won or lost a basketball game. David, what's wrong with you? We don't belong here. We ought to be—"

"Okay—okay." He didn't want to listen to her any longer. "I'm going to find Mark. This is your last chance to come with me. Are you coming?"

"I want my father."

"We'll talk about that later. We tell Mark first. Are you coming?"

"No."

"Then sit here and wait. I'll be back in a minute. *We'll* be back in a minute."

He left the car and half walked, half ran across the parking lot. People were pouring out of the doorways to the gym. He had to stand on the edge of the flood, working his way in between two outward-rushing people, then between another pair. Somebody shouted, "Hey, Dave, where are you going?" Somebody else gave him a hard shove in the ribs with an elbow, muttering, "The tide goes in the other direction, good buddy."

Mark—where was Mark? David worked his way down an aisle. The crowd was thinning now and there was nobody left on the gym floor. The score was still posted on the board, home team, 61, visitors, 57. Del

Norte had won, then, as usual. There was no way any-body defeated Jeff when he charged down the court, a head taller than anyone else; that ball under absolute control. Why couldn't the rest of life be controlled so easily? How could things get out of hand so quickly?

Mark—Mark—where are you?

Then he saw him at last, down at the end of the court in front of the door to the locker room, standing with Betsy. Dave broke into a run, his eyes trained on them, unable to see anything except the two figures.

"Mark!" He opened his mouth to shout the name, but no sound emerged. "Mark—Mark—Mark—" His lips kept moving, but nothing came from between them. They saw him now. Both of hem had turned toward him, Betsy with her lips parted, her eyes wide and astonished. "Why, it's David!"

Mark's face was inscrutable. "Yeah, it's David. Well, boy, how goes it? Something the matter?"

"He's dead," David said. He had not meant to state it so abruptly. The words flew out of him, escaping from his throat and over the top of his tongue be-fore he could stop them, before he could weigh what he was saying. "He's dead."

There was a moment's silence. Then Mark said, "Griffin?"

"Yes."

"How do you know?"

"Sue and I went up there. We looked at him. There's no guessing about it, Mark; he's gone. He's—gone." How could one describe those eyes staring up-ward into the far reaching, incredible space of the night sky? "He's dead, Mark."

"I believe you."

Betsy was staring at both of them, speechless.

"Where's Sue?" Mark asked. "Why isn't she with you?"

"She's out in the car."

"In the lot, here?"

"Yes."

"Then get out there, boy! She might take off across the place and yell to a pig. She's all spaced out, that chick. Run, now! I mean it!"

"Aren't you coming?"

"Sure, I'm coming. I've got to wait for Jeff. Betsy, you go with Dave. Do something about Sue. You know how she'll go—a total basket case." He reached out suddenly and touched Betsy's cheek, his hand light, almost but not quite a caress.

"Hey, girl, I'm counting on you."

"Yes—okay." Betsy's eyes were huge in her round face. "David said—I mean, it's not true, is it? It can't be, can it? Mark, he's not really—I mean—"

"Get going, will you? Nobody needs to see us standing together like this. Jeff will be out in a minute, and we'll come join you."

They went.

They crossed the corner of the gym floor together, David's hand placed protectively beneath Betsy's elbow. A few people turned—turned back—smiled at each other. Guess what? A new romance! The senior class president and the head cheerleader, what a perfect combination! Why hadn't it happened sooner?

"You didn't mean it, did you, David? It's all a joke, isn't it?"

"A real funny one," David said numbly. He tightened his grip on her elbow until his nails bit into her flesh and she jerked away from him. Where am I? he asked himself in bewilderment. What am I doing here? Where has the night gone? It's a dream, that's all, one of those crazy dreams that seem so real and yet you know all the time down underneath that in a minute you'll wake up. A moment ago it was six o'clock—we were eating dinner, Mother and Gram and I—and then I went out—and I stopped at Susan's—and then—and then—

They reached the door to the outside. Now they were through it, walking together across the parking lot. Where was the car?

"Over there," David said. "That's it—over there." It was the only car parked alone and unmoving amid the turmoil of flaring lights and sounding horns. Sue was still in it. He could see her profile outlined against the lights of the cars beyond. Her head was turned at a right angle with her eyes focused on the gym doors. Her chin was high. She was still not crying. Even before entering the car he could tell that by the lift of her chin.

They reached the car and opened the door and climbed in. Susan turned, her glance going past David, past Betsy.

"Where's Mark?"

"Coming. He had to wait for Jeff."

"You said you'd get him. Did you tell him?"

"Yes. He'll be along in a minute."

"Are you okay, Sue?" Betsy asked. "You're not going to go to pieces or anything, are you? You look like you're okay."

"Here they come," David said with relief. "That's Jeff, see—over there against the lights? Mark must have dragged him out before he hit the showers."

"Did you tell him?" Susan asked again.

"I said I did, didn't I?" Her calm was frightening to him because it was so unnatural. He reached out for her and could not find her hand. He wished suddenly

that he could throw himself across the seat that lay
between them and put his arms around her and hold
her and tell her to go ahead and cry and cry. Cry for
herself, and for him too, for Mr. Griffin alone on the
bank of the mountain stream, for all of them.

Jeff and Mark were closer now, a tall figure and a
shorter one, working their way across the lot. Eventu-
ally they reached the car, and Mark opened the front
door on the far side.

"Shove over," he said. "Move over, Sue, I'm getting
in beside you. Dave, you get this thing going. Jeff, get
in back with Betsy."

"Where do you want to go?" David asked.

"Anywhere," Mark said. "Give me a minute and I'll
think of a place. Meanwhile, just drive. Get us out of
here."

David started the engine and drove out of the lot
and turned east on Montgomery. After they had gone
a few miles Mark said, "Pull in there." It was a lot
behind a row of apartment buildings, and David
steered the car carefully into it and drew to a stop behind a garbage bin. He turned off the key, and there
was silence.

For a moment no one spoke. Then Mark drew a
long breath.

"Well," he said, "it looks like your dream came
true, Jeff, old boy. We 'killed Mr. Griffin' for real."

"We didn't!" Jeff said. "We didn't do anything to
him. Nobody's going to stick this on me! I hardly
touched him!"

"Nobody can stick it on any of us," Mark said.
"We've got our alibis. Dave was with his grandmother
all afternoon watching television. You and I were at
Betsy's."

"We've got that solid," Betsy said. "The woman

next door phoned Mom tonight while we were eating dinner and complained about how we played records so loud we woke her kid up from his nap."

"And tonight most of us were at the game. People saw us there. The best thing now is to show up at the Snack-'n-Soda as usual and then hit it for home."

"You mean—not_ *tell* anybody?" Susan said in amazement.

"Why should we do that?"

"Why, because—because—there's a man *dead!*"

"Would he be any less dead if we told people?"

"No, of course not. But you can't just have somebody die and not report it."

"If we reported it, we'd have to tell about the kidnapping," Jeff said. "Who'd believe us when we explained how we were just having a little fun? They'd check over his body, and there'd be bruises on him where he fell down, and maybe the ropes have made cuts on his arms and legs. Whatever happened to make him die, that would be blamed on us too, even though we didn't have a darned thing to do with it. We could end up in jail."

"We're minors," Betsy reminded him. "Minors can't be jailed, can they? Besides, my dad's on the County Commission."

"Hold it, Bets," Mark said. "We wouldn't be considered minors now."

"What do you mean?" Betsy asked in bewilderment. "We're all of us underage."

"If somebody's killed during the commission of a felony, it's first degree murder," Mark said. "Kidnapping's a felony. No matter what our ages, we'd be tried as adults."

"But—that's not fair!" exclaimed Betsy. "Besides, it wasn't a real kidnapping! It was a joke!"

"Who's going to believe that?" Jeff asked. "We could spend the rest of our lives in jail! And talking about your dad, think what this would do to him. It would be all over the papers—'County Commissioner's daughter indicted for murder.' Christ!"

"And my mother." David felt a wave of nausea hit his stomach. "There's no way I could tell my mother."

"We *have* to tell!" Susan insisted. "We don't have a choice! People will be looking for him! Mrs. Griffin will call the police, and Mr. Griffin won't show up to teach tomorrow, and everybody will know he's missing."

"Lots of people turn up missing," Mark said. "It happens every day. Right, Dave?"

David nodded. "They do. Men leave home. They go—just light out and go—and years go by, and nobody ever finds out where they went. Their wives go on all right. It's tough, maybe, but they make out."

His own mother's face rose up before him, the lines etched deep around the corners of the eyes and mouth. A "saint," the Reverend Chandler had called her. She had liked that. Not every woman had the chance to become a saint. It was rough, of course, but was it really any worse than being a widow?

"We're clean as soon as we get rid of two things," Mark said, "the body and the car. Once those are gone there's nothing left to worry about. We can't do anything tonight, it's too dark and too late. And we can't cut school tomorrow. It'll have to be tomorrow afternoon. Who can get hold of a shovel?"

"I can," Jeff said. "We've got one in the garage."

"What about an extra license plate?"

Silence followed the question. Then Jeff said, "Maybe Tony—"

"No way," Mark said firmly. "We're not letting anybody else in on this. There are too many of us involved already. If we take the north road down from the mountains we can come into town via Coors Road. That should be pretty safe if we time it to hit the evening traffic. All those people who work in the Levi and Singer factories come home that way. We'll be part of the swarm."

"And then what?" Betsy asked. "Once we get the car back to town, what do we do with it?"

"We can park it at the airport. That lot's always full, and cars get left there for months at a time. When they do find it, if they do, it will look like Griffin took a plane someplace."

"And—the body?" David forced out the question. "You're planning for us to bury it?"

"That's simple enough. Right where it is now is a perfect place. Nobody ever goes there, and the dirt will be soft because of the stream."

"No!" The word burst from Susan's lips like a cry of pain. "We can't do that, just take Mr. Griffin and stick him in the ground! We can't pretend it never happened, that we're not reponsible! We killed him, all five of us! Somehow we killed him! I don't know how, but if we hadn't done what we did, he would still be alive this minute!"

"You can't know that," Mark said reasonably.

"I do know it! People don't just fall down dead for no reason!"

"And they don't 'just fall down dead' from being tied up for a few hours."

"I don't care what you say, we've got to tell somebody! My father—"

"Sue—sue—simmer down, baby." Mark's voice was

suddenly gentle. "I know how you feel. You and Dave were the ones who found him. That was rough, and that's over now. You don't have to go up there again. The rest of us will take care of everything. It's going to be all right, baby, I promise."

"It can't be all right!" Susan cried miserably. "Mr. Griffin is dead!"

"Did you stop to think he might be dead regardless?" Mark placed his hand under her chin, turning her face to his. "Look, sweetie, we didn't do the guy in, and you know it. Dolly Luna got kidnapped by her students last semester, right? She didn't fall dead on them. It's a sick person who dies like that, without a reason. It could have happened anywhere—in his home, behind his desk at school, walking down the street—when your body quits on you, that's it. Wouldn't it have been worse if he had been behind the wheel of his car and plowed straight into a bunch of kids waiting for the school bus?"

"If he had been at home his wife could have called a doctor," Susan said.

"My own dad was at home when he died," Mark said softly. "It would have been better if he hadn't been. He was in his bed asleep, and the house burned down."

"Oh, Mark!" She regarded him with horror. "How awful!"

"Darned right, it was awful. The point is, when it's your time to go, you go. You can't keep saying 'if this' and 'if that'; it doesn't change anything. You can't go back and change anything, you've just got to keep on living. Wrecking our own lives wouldn't bring Mr. G. back, now would it? It wouldn't help at all. It would just destroy us and the people who love us."

"My parents couldn't bear it," Susan said. "Nothing

like this ever happens to people like my parents. They're so nice and normal. They just think about things like cooking and property taxes."

"They don't have to know. Nobody does. It's all right, Sue." He put his arm around her shoulders and pulled her over against him. "It's all right, Sue—Susie—it's all right, baby. Just trust old Mark, okay? It's all going to be all right."

The tears came at last with the suddenness of a dam bursting, one gigantic sob that seemed to shake the car, and then the wild, heavy weeping. Mark's other arm came around her, and he held her through the storm, his face still and impassive, the heavy-lidded eyes half-closed, staring out through the front car window into the darkness beyond.

He held her that way for a long time.

When the weeping slowed, he turned to David. "Do you have a handkerchief?"

David did, in his back pants pocket. He dug it out and handed it to Susan, who took off her glasses and wiped her eyes and blew her nose.

"Let's head for the Snack-'n-Soda," Mark said to David. "We'll hang around there just long enough to have a Coke so people will see us. Then we'll go home."

TEN

"Is he gone already?" Irv Kinney asked.

His wife Jeanne glanced up from her coffee and nodded a pin-curled head.

"Jeff came by for him earlier than usual this morning. He was honking the car horn out there at seven-thirty, and Mark was out the door before I could even ask him if he'll be here for dinner."

"Why should he be here for dinner?" Irv asked her, getting a bowl out of the cabinet and opening the top of the new box of breakfast cereal. "Sometimes I wonder if the kid lives here at all. Days go by and I never see him. He sleeps in till his friend blows the horn for him in the mornings, and he doesn't come home at night till after we're in bed. Where does he eat, anyway?"

"I think he picks up hamburgers," Jeanne said. "You know how kids are."

"I know how *our* kids were, and it wasn't like that. We had our ups and downs with them, sure, but they sat down at the dinner table with us like they be-

longed to the family, and we saw enough of them evenings and weekends to remember what they looked
like from one month to the next. Mark's been living
with us four years now, and I swear, I don't think
we've ever had a conversation."

"Our kids were real outgoing. Everybody's not the
same."

"That's for sure." Irv carried the cereal bowl over to
the table and sat down with it. He reached for the
milk carton. "Sometimes I wonder if we did the right
thing, taking him in like that. We raised our family
once, and starting all over again at our ages—what
made us think we could do it?"

"We didn't have much choice, did we, with your
brother Pete dead and Eva with a nervous breakdown?
Mark was only thirteen. He's your nephew. Who else
would have taken him?"

"That's it, of course. There wasn't anybody but us. I
kept thinking Eva would come around after the shock
was over. Still, if we'd said no, the courts would have
had to come up with something for him, a foster
home, maybe, with people there who were used to han-
dling weird kids."

"Mark's not weird," Jeanne said. "You keep com-
paring him to our kids, and you just can't do that and
be fair about it. He's gone through things they never
had to go through. Imagine, seeing his own house
burn down with his father inside it, and then having
his mother crack up and turn on him like that and say
she never wanted to see him again—why, that's
enough to make any boy—different."

" 'Weird'—'different'—what does it matter what
word you use? What it boils down to is that the kid
gives me the creeps. I say that, even if he is my brother's boy. I've tried to reach him, Jeanne. You know

that. You remember how I stuck up for him after he got in that trouble at school? I went in with him and stood behind him and tried to get them to give him another chance in another English class."

"He appreciated that, Irv."

"Did he? I never could tell. Why did he do that anyway, crib on that paper? He's smart enough. He didn't need to do that."

"Maybe his girl friend put him up to it. She was older than he was. Young boys can be influenced a lot by girls like that."

"Where does he go nights, that's what I want to know. You ask him, and he says, 'Nowhere much.' Now, what kind of answer is that—'nowhere much'? Last night I heard the front door open and close around eleven-thirty. That's the earliest he's come in all month. You don't think he's into drugs or something, do you, Jeanne?"

"I don't know any better than you do," his wife said. "If he is, there's nothing we can do about it, so what's the sense agonizing? He's almost eighteen. He'll be graduating in another month or so. There'll be enough left from his father's insurance so he can make out until he gets his feet on the ground. You and I will always know we did the right thing."

"I guess you're right," Irv said with a sigh. "I just have this feeling—" He let the sentence fall away, incomplete. "I wonder if he'll keep in touch with us after he leaves."

"Probably not," Jeanne said, taking a sip of coffee.

"You're not eating much this morning," David's mother commented at breakfast. "Are you upset about something, David? You and your friend didn't have a fuss last night, did you?"

"No," David said. "We met up with some friends and went out with them for food around eleven. My stomach's still full from that."

"You were out awfully late for a school night," his mother said. "I hope this isn't going to become a regular thing. You know I need my sleep, and there's no way I'm going to get it if I'm worrying about you out driving around till all hours."

"I'm sorry. It won't happen again."

To please her, he picked up a slice of toast and took a bite out of it. The bread was hard and dry and crumbly, and the butter felt slimy on his tongue. He was afraid he couldn't swallow it. He picked up his glass of milk and took a gulp, willing the mouthful down.

"I can't believe it—our little Davy dating." His grandmother regarded him fondly from her place at the end of the kitchen table, her gray hair still uncombed, her flowered robe hanging open to reveal the pink cotton nightgown her daughter-in-law had given her for Christmas. "Young people grow up so fast these days. Why, on that game show with the newlyweds, you'd swear there wasn't a one of them any older than sixteen."

"I'm *seventeen,*" David reminded her automatically.

"Yes, I know, dear. You told me that yesterday. Or was it yesterday? One does lose track of time when one gets old. Yesterday was the day you went out with that boy with the funny eyes and rode around with him and his friends and never came home till dinner."

"It was *not!*" David set his glass down so hard that the milk splashed over onto the table top. "I came straight home from school yesterday. I got you a Jell-O, and you and I sat all afternoon and watched television. You do remember that, don't you, Gram? *That* was yesterday."

"It was?" The old woman reached up a wrinkled hand to shove a strand of hair back from her forehead. "I get confused. One day gets to be the same size as the next when you're my age."

"You're not *that* old; you can remember." David's voice rose sharply. "Yesterday was Thursday, right? It was Wednesday I went out with Mark and the other kids for a while. Yesterday—Thursday—I came right home from school and got you the green Jell-O I'd made that morning for you, and you ate it, and I turned the television on, and we sat there together all afternoon long. I was right in the room with you all afternoon."

"David, for goodness sake," his mother said. "You don't have to shout at Gram that way."

"I want her to remember!"

"I remember—I remember." Old Mrs. Ruggles nodded agreeably. "I remember the green Jell-O, after all those weeks with the yellow stuff. Where's the rest of it, Davy? I want some for breakfast."

"There isn't any more," David said. "You finished it."

"A whole package? She couldn't have," his mother exclaimed. "That makes four bowls."

"Well, I ate some of them."

"You didn't," his grandmother contradicted. "I do remember now. You didn't eat any of it. I asked you if you were going to eat something, and you said no, you weren't hungry. Maybe you dumped the rest of the Jell-O out because it tasted funny."

"Why would it taste funny?" David's mother asked. "Jell-O is Jell-O. It's all the same. That's the same powder in every box."

"It tasted great," David said. "That's why I ate all the rest of it. I just got started and I couldn't stop, and I ate it all, and I washed out the bowls and dried them and put them away. Is that a crime, being hungry after school?"

"You didn't eat them," his grandmother said stubbornly. "I would have seen you do it."

"You were asleep! You fell asleep almost as soon as I turned the TV on. Admit it, now, you don't remember anything at all about the shows, now do you? What were the questions they asked the newlyweds? Can you tell me?"

"They asked about—about—" The old woman closed her eyes and wrinkled her forehead. "Goodness, I don't recall at all. Did I really sleep? I never sleep in the daytime. But, you're right, I ate that Jell-O and I just went right to sleep like Snow White did when the queen gave her the poison apple. You didn't give me a poison Jell-O, did you, Davy?" She opened her eyes and laughed delightedly at her witticism.

"I told you, I ate all the rest of it. If there had been something in the Jell-O, I'd have gone to sleep too, wouldn't I?" He seemed suddenly to have no control over his voice. It was rising higher and higher.

His mother was staring at him in bewilderment.

"Please, dear, don't *yell!* I've never seen you act like this, David. Gram was joking about the Jell-O, of course. And there's nothing wrong with catching a little nap in the afternoons, Mother Ruggles. I'd do it myself if I were home and able to."

"But I missed my shows," Irma Ruggles said mournfully. "I like that girl with the curly hair who won two days now. I wanted to see her win again. Did she, Davy?"

"Yes," David said desperately. "Yes, she won. They gave her an electric mixer."

"Only a mixer? The third time winning, they usually give them something really big like a new refrigerator."

"They offered her one, but she said she didn't want it. She already had a refrigerator. She wanted a mixer."

"But if she'd taken the refrigerator she could have sold it and bought the mixer and had money left over. They ought to think of things like that, those young people, but they're just not very sensible. It takes an older head to figure things out." She paused and then asked, "Is there another package of that Jell-O you could make up for me?"

"There certainly is," David's mother said. "I bought some yesterday. David will make it before he leaves for school, won't you, dear, and it will be all ready by this afternoon."

"Sure, Gram," David said, weak with relief at the turn the conversation had taken. "I'll be glad to."

"That will be nice, dear." His grandmother smiled at him benignly. "And this time, Davy, be very careful what you put in it, won't you? That last stuff was awfully bitter."

"I want to talk to Detective James Baca."

"Can you tell me what the problem is, ma'am?" the young man at the front desk asked pleasantly.

"My husband's missing," Kathy Griffin told him. "I phoned here last night and talked to somebody—I'm not sure who—and he said to come in this morning and ask for Detective Baca."

"Your name, please?"

"Katherine Griffin."

"One moment, please." The young man picked up
his phone, dialed an extension, and spoke quietly into
the receiver. Then he replaced it on the hook. "Go on
down the hall, ma'am. Room one-oh-seven."

"Thank you."

Clutching her purse tightly against the front of her
maternity blouse, Kathy walked down the hall, counting doorways, 103—105—107. The door stood par-
tially open, and she gave it a push and stepped inside.

The man seated in a captain's chair behind the
large, paper-covered desk was stocky and broad-
shouldered, his black hair streaked with gray. He did
not rise when she came in but glanced up, nodded,
and gestured toward a chair beside his desk.

"Sit down, Mrs. Griffin. I got the message about
your call last night. Your husband still hasn't turned
up?"

"No," Kathy said, sinking into the chair, her hands
tightening convulsively around the purse. "There
hasn't been a word. I'm about out of my mind."

"How long has he been missing?"

"He didn't come home from work yesterday," Kathy
told him. "I called the principal last night—Brian's a
teacher at Del Norte—and he said Brian was there for
all his classes. It's as though in the few miles between
the school and our house, he vanished into thin air."

"Okay. Let's get some basic information down and
then we can see where to go from there." The detective
drew out a pad of letter-sized forms and picked up a
pen. "Your husband's full name and address?"

"Brian Joseph Griffin, Ten-twenty Ashwood, North-
east."

"His age and place of birth?"

"Brian's forty-one. He was born here in Albuquerque."

"Would you describe him for me, please?"

"He's—oh, about five foot ten or so, I guess. He's slender. His hair's dark, almost black, and he wears it short. He has blue eyes and wears glasses. He has a mustache."

"Do you know his Social Security number?"

"No, not offhand. Is that important?"

"Not necessarily, but it helps because it's an identifying number. It might be the same as his service number. Was he in the service?"

"No," Kathy said. "He has a heart problem that kept him out."

"What sort of problem?"

"Angina. It's a circulatory thing; sometimes the muscles around the heart clutch up and not enough oxygen gets through. It's painful, but it's controllable, not like a real heart attack. All he has to do is take a pill."

"Does your husband get these attacks often?"

"Usually they come when he's tense and under pressure. He can feel one coming on, and if he takes a pill immediately he can prevent it. But it was enough of a problem to keep him out of the service."

"Where did Brian go to college, Mrs. Griffin?"

"Stanford University."

"Does he have any scars or marks, any tattoos—that sort of thing?"

"No," Kathy said.

"And he's been missing since yesterday afternoon. Is that correct?"

"Yes. He was supposed to have a conference after school with one of his pupils. Susan—McConnell, I think her name is. That would have made him a little later than usual. And then—oh, I forgot this, he was going to stop at Skagg's Pharmacy to pick up a prescription for his nitroglycerin pills. I don't know if he ever did that. All I know is he didn't come home."

"Has he ever done anything like this before?" Detective Baca asked her. "Gone away for a period of time without telling you?"

"Never. Brian's always called me if he was going to be even a little late."

"Has he been worried about anything lately? Has he seemed preoccupied with his work or anything else?"

"No more than usual. Brian's very serious about his teaching, and he worries a lot over lesson plans and criticizing assignments, but—no—actually I think he's been more lighthearted than usual. He's excited about the baby."

"Is this your first child?" Detective Baca asked her.

"Yes, it is. We got married later than lots of people, and then Brian wanted to wait to start a family until he knew his teaching was going to work out. He used to be a college professor, and he switched over into high-school teaching, and he wanted to be sure he could handle it." Her voice broke. "Brian's always so precise about everything. I can't believe he would do this. Something terrible must have happened to him."

"There may be a perfectly logical answer," the detective said. "Let me ask you a couple more questions. Is there anyone, a close relative or friend, whom your husband might contact if he should be in any kind of difficulty?"

"I can't think who," Kathy said. "His parents are dead and he doesn't have brothers or sisters. Brian is a very self-contained man. Since he stopped teaching at the university he's more or less lost touch with people there. You know how the college social structure goes; it's awfully groupy."

"You don't do any socializing together?"

"Oh, we sometimes have my old friends from work over with their husbands, or maybe some of the neighborhood couples, but it's very casual, just bridge once in a while or something like that. And they're more my friends than Brian's. The most important people in Brian's life, besides me, are his students."

Detective Baca set down his pen and leaned back in his chair.

"That's it for formal questions. Now, tell me, where do *you* think your husband might be, Mrs. Griffin. Do you have any ideas?"

Kathy shook her head miserably. "I've racked my brain trying to come up with a logical explanation. The first thing I did, of course, was phone the hospitals in case there had been an accident, but nobody of Brian's description had been brought in."

"Does Brian drink?"

"Never. In fact, he's allergic to alcohol."

"Does he have any enemies? Has he ever been involved in anything unlawful?"

"No. No."

"How are things between the two of you?" Baca asked her. "It's not unusual for a first pregnancy to cause waves in a marriage. It means a whole new way of living. The honeymoon's over; the escape hatch is no longer open, even a crack. Some pretty good men have been known to go into panic during that period of life, and your husband has gone forty-one years before being hit with fatherhood."

"You're implying Brian may just have run away?" Kathy shook her head violently. "That's impossible."

"I don't mean to offend you," the man across from her said quietly. "It's just that we've had three husbands reported missing in the past month, and in every case the wife's been pregnant. One man got as far as his mother's place in Arizona, had second thoughts, and turned around and came back.

"The second guy is still gone, but his wife got a postcard from him from California. He wants her to file for divorce. But, they'd had a number of problems with their marriage to start with. It does happen, Mrs. Griffin."

"Not with Brian."

"One final question. What was the last thing your husband said to you before he left for work yesterday? Do you remember?"

"He said, 'I love you.'" There was a note of hard pride in Kathy's voice. "Brian did not run out on me, Mr. Baca. He's not that sort of person. It just is not possible."

"Then there has to be another answer," the big man said gently. "People don't disappear 'into thin air,' as you put it. Your husband is somewhere, and we'll do everything we can to locate him.

"To start things off, I'd like to talk with that student at the high school, the one who may have been the last person to see him yesterday."

ELEVEN

"Susan McConnell—come to the office, please!"

The loudspeaker in the ceiling over the door blared the words throughout the room, and Susan, sitting hunched over her history notebook, felt her heart drop into her stomach with a sickening thud. It was the moment she had been anticipating ever since she had arrived at school that morning to see Dolly Luna, bright faced and cheerful, perched on the corner of Mr. Griffin's desk.

"Mr. Griffin isn't here this morning," she had explained. "So I'm subbing for him. I haven't been able to find his notes for today's class, so we'll just have to play it by ear, I guess. You'll have to tell me where you are in the book, and maybe we can read aloud or something."

She had smiled brightly.

"My name's Miss Luna, but if you promise not to tell anybody, I'll let you call me Dolly."

And so they had read—or, rather, Dolly had read, her lilting voice carrying Ophelia gaily through her tunnels of madness to her ultimate watery end—and Susan had thought, this can't be real. It's a cartoon—a dream—a nightmare. That's it—it's a nightmare. Soon I will wake up and I'll be at home in my bed with one of the twins banging at the door to tell me I've overslept, and I'll open my eyes, and the sun will be pouring through the window onto the rug and outside in the elm tree birds will be singing.

But she had already awakened to that scene an hour before, and one could not wake up twice. Actually, she could not believe that she had slept at all. When she had gone to bed the night before, she had thought, I will never sleep, and then exhaustion had rolled upon her in a gigantic, smothering wave, and she had sunk gratefully beneath it. A moment later, it seemed, Francis had been at the door, calling in to her, "Sue! Are you alive in there? Mom wants to know if you're feeling good enough to go to school this morning."

"Yes—I am—I'll be right down," Susan had mumbled, opening her eyes to the sunlight and the birdsong and the terrible realization that tomorrow had arrived.

She had gotten up and gone into the bathroom and washed her face, pressing the cold washcloth for long moments against her swollen eyelids and puffy cheeks. I must have cried in my sleep, she thought. I must have cried all night.

When she entered the kitchen the whole family was at the breakfast table. Her mother glanced up worriedly.

"Your cold must be worse, Sue. You look just awful. Are you sure you want to go to school?"

"I feel fine," Susan told her. "You don't miss school, just for a little cold."

"I would," Melvynne said. "I'd miss school for anything. Huh, Fran?"

"Me too," Francis said. "Even for nothing, I'd miss school."

"Well, your sister isn't like you two," Mr. McConnell said approvingly. "She takes her education seriously. If you boys would straighten up and follow her example, we'd have a happier household around here at grading time."

"Sue's a girl," Craig said. "Most girls are grinds. Guys are different. They've got other things on their minds."

"My guess would be that David Ruggles makes good grades," Mrs. McConnell said. "You don't get to be president of the senior class on D's and F's. Right, Sue?"

"Yes," Susan said, "David does well in school." It was a strange situation finding herself on top for a change, being held up to the boys as an example to follow. Normally she would have been delighted. Today she felt ashamed and sickened.

If they knew—if they had any idea—what sort of person I really am, she thought miserably, they would never, any of them, want anything to do with me again.

She would have given anything at that moment to have said, "You're right, I am too sick to go to school," and left the table and gone upstairs and crawled back into bed with her face buried in the pillow and the covers pulled up over her head, blocking out the world. But the last thing Mark had said to them was, "You guys show up for school tomorrow. We don't want to draw attention to ourselves by being absent. The whole bunch of us are going to be in Griffin's class, just like it was any old day, and we'll be as surprised as the rest of them when he doesn't show. Get me?"

And when Mark told you something, you did it. She could understand now what David had meant when he had told her, "Mark isn't like other people." There was a strength in Mark, an ability to know exactly what to do in any emergency, and when Mark said something, you had to believe it, because if you couldn't believe in Mark, you couldn't believe in anything. "Trust me—trust old Mark," he had told her last night, his arms a comforting fortress around her. "Everything's going to be all right."

Mark knew; he *had* to know. If they did exactly what he told them, things would somehow work out and the terrible present would one day lie behind them and be the past, and people could forget the past if they tried to. But it was important, terribly important, to do precisely as Mark said.

And so she ate what she could of breakfast and collected her books and left for school with the boys, parting with them at the corner to continue down Montgomery to Del Norte while the twins turned off toward the grammar school and Craig toward the junior high.

"Hope you feel better, sis," Craig said, surprisingly, as they split forces, giving her a look of actual concern, and she had murmured, "Thanks. I'm sure I will."

But she had not been prepared for the appearance of Dolly Luna on Mr. Griffin's desk top. He would have hated it, she thought, just hated it to hear her hacking up *Hamlet*. She had sat with her head bowed over her book, almost ready to believe that the door might fly open and Mr. Griffin come striding in to take his rightful place and send Dolly flying off to the teacher's lounge for her morning coffee.

We cannot get away with it, she told herself. No matter what Mark says, somehow we'll be found out. Any minute now a policeman will appear at the door or the speaker will call our names.

Which was why she was not surprised when she heard it at last in history class.

"Susan McConnell, come to the office, please!"

Susan raised her head. Two dozen pairs of eyes turned to stare at her.

Mr. Stanton, the history teacher, nodded his permission.

"In case you're not back before the end of the period, the assignment is to read the next chapter and answer the questions at the end."

Wordlessly, Susan got to her feet, collecting her history book, her notebook, a ball-point pen, her purse. Will they let me go to my locker for my jacket, she wondered? It hardly mattered. The cold gripping her came from within and no layer of outer clothing would ever alleviate it.

She crossed the room and went through the door out into the hallway.

Mark was leaning against the wall by the water fountain.

"What are you doing here?" Susan asked him.

"Waiting for you."

"Did they call you too?" Susan asked him.

"Nope."

"Any of the others?"

"No. You're the chosen one."

"Then, how did you know—"

"I sit by the window facing the parking lot," Mark said. "I've been keeping my eye out for a squad car. I was pretty sure when they got the report Mr. G. was missing they'd send somebody over here to check things out. This is the last place he was seen, and you're the last person to have seen him, so it stands to reason they're going to want to ask you some questions. I've got a biology lab this period, so I slid out of the room and came down to see how you were holding up."

"I'm scared," Susan said. "I don't know what to tell them. If they've found out everything—"

"They haven't found out anything," Mark said. "Not one blasted thing, and don't you forget it. All they know is that Mr. G. didn't go home last night and didn't come to work this morning. That's it— that's *all*. Nothing else. The only way they're going to find out anything else is if you tell them."

"They'll ask me questions—"

"And you'll give them answers. You've got nothing to hide, right? So tell them the truth. You wanted a conference with Mr. G. to talk about your grade on that last test. You met him when school let out. You talked about—what? Whatever it was, tell them. There's no reason to hide anything there."

"He said I was bright enough, but sloppy. That I messed myself up by not paying attention to details. He said that in his class an A meant 'perfect,' and that nobody in that class including me was doing perfect work, but that I was probably capable of it if I made the effort."

"Okay. What else?"

"He said that I was spoiled—that we were all spoiled—because we're used to overgrading. That so few high-school students take their work seriously that anybody who seems to be doing *anything* stands out, and teachers reward them with A's, even though they don't deserve them, because they're better than the others. And because they get A's, they think they're doing great, and they never even try to push themselves into doing the best work they can possibly do."

"That sounds like him, the bastard. F's for everybody so they'll try harder. Anything else?"

"Not really. We talked about the test—where I had made mistakes and stuff like that—and some about Shakespeare—what he meant by certain lines that I hadn't understood. When it was over and we started to leave, he started talking about Hamlet's feeling of guilt over Ophelia's death and whether or not that really changed him as a person. That's why I had to walk out to the parking lot with him. I hadn't meant to, but I couldn't just say 'So long' and walk away from him when he was in the middle of a sentence, and he seemed to take it for granted that I was going out that way."

"So you walked him out to the lot, and then?"

"He asked if he could give me a ride home."

"No, he didn't."

"He—didn't?" Susan asked blankly.

"Nope. He had other plans, and taking you home would have interfered with them. In fact, all the while you were having your conference, he acted sort of peculiar. He kept checking his watch and glancing out the window. Sometimes you'd ask him a question, and he'd act like he didn't hear it. His mind was on something else."

"But, that's not true," Susan said.

"Sure, it's true. How else would a guy act who had a woman on his mind?"

"I don't understand."

"When you walked out to the parking lot with the guy, you started off in the direction of home, and then something about the way he'd been acting made you look back. He was getting into his car, and there was a woman in it."

"But there wasn't!"

"A real doll, blond and foxy. Young—maybe twenty-two or so, and really sexy. Sitting up front, right next to the driver's seat."

"I can't say a thing like that," Susan exclaimed.

"Of course, you can. You can say anything you want to. You're the last one who saw him, aren't you? Who else is going to know who was in that car? You're the one who saw him get into it and drive away."

"But why?" Susan asked. "Why make up something like that? What good will it do?"

"It'll lead them away from us. Right now, who do they have to suspect of having a hand in this? Students. Maybe not us, exactly, but students in general; who else did Mr. G. have in his life? And when they start going over the students in his classes, they're going to zero in on a few people who've had some bad problems with him. That means me. And maybe Jeff. And once they hit on us, it'll follow pretty quick that the rest of you get nailed too.

"So what do we do? We throw in a foxy lady, and right away there's a whole new look to things. There's a secret part of Mr. G.'s life that nobody knows about. Who is this chick? Where did she come from? How come they were driving off together? Who's going to think about students when there's a love interest to worry over?"

"I can't do that, Mark," Susan said shakily. "Mr. Griffin was married, you know. How would his wife feel, hearing something like that? She'd think—"

"She'd think he ran out on her. What's so bad about that? It's a kindness, baby. If she loved the guy—and it's hard to believe anyone could—wouldn't she rather think of him off having a good time someplace, even if it wasn't with her, than *dead?*"

"Well— when you put it like that—"

"You'd better get moving. We've been standiing here talking five minutes, and they're down there at the office waiting for you."

"Mark, come with me!" Susan said pleadingly. "I just can't do it by myself. We could say you were with me after school—that you waited for me till the conference was over—that you and I *both* saw the woman in the car."

"No way," Mark said firmly. "You're Miss Innocence. Stick me in the picture, and we've lost the ball game. You can do it, Sue. You'll do just great."

"I'm scared!"

"Don't be. It'll be simple as pie. A girl like you—who's going to doubt her? Now, on with the show, baby, and remember—I'm counting on you." He laid his hand briefly on her shoulder.

"I'll try." Susan drew in a long breath. "And after school?"

"You just go on home like you would on any other day. This is your part now. When you've carried this through, it's over. The rest of us will take care of the other part—the bit in the mountains and moving the car and whatever. Okay?"

"Okay," Susan said. "If you say so, Mark."

She took a few steps down the hall and stopped abruptly as he said, "Sue?"

"What?"

"Relax, will you? Don't walk in there looking like you're facing a firing squad. Remember, you don't know a thing about why they're calling you. It might be for something great, like telling you you're going to be named student of the year."

He stood quietly watching with narrowed eyes as she continued down the hall to the office door. She paused and looked back at him. He raised his hand in a small encouraging wave.

Susan opened the door and went inside.

"Christ," Mark said softly under his breath. He bent over the fountain and took a drink.

TWELVE

At three-thirty the four of them got into Jeff's car and drove into the mountains. The afternoon was warm and still, and the air that poured in through the open windows smelled of pine needles and sunshine.

"Don't you feel like you were playing the same scene twice?" Jeff asked. "It's like last Saturday all over again. You're even all sitting in the same places in the car."

"I wish it *were* last Saturday," David said wistfully. "I wish we could go back to then and start all over."

"There's one nice difference," said Betsy. "The creep's not with us. How come you let her slide out, Mark? She's in this as much as the rest of us. Why doesn't she have to do some of the dirty work too?"

"She couldn't take it," Mark said.

"So you're babying her? That's not fair." Betsy's mouth puckered into a pout. "If Sue can get out of this part, why shouldn't I? I'm a girl too."

"It's not that," Mark said impatiently. "There's no 'fair' about it. It's just that Sue's at the freak-out point, and it's not going to take much to push her over. If she does crack, she runs and tells her father the whole blasted story. Besides, she's done her bit today. She had a scene with the pigs this morning."

"I hope she didn't blow it," Jeff muttered.

"She didn't. I talked with her afterward. She fed them exactly what I told her to."

"Who couldn't do that?" Betsy said. "It doesn't take an Academy Award-winning actress. With that soft little voice of hers and those big, nearsighted cow eyes blinking behind those glasses—"

"Cut it," David broke in sharply. "Don't rake her over that way."

"Why not, for Pete's sake? Don't tell me you've gone soft on her, I'll never believe it! Not *you*—not *her*—it's impossible!"

"She's a nice girl."

"Oh, I'm sure she is. So nice she can't dirty her hands digging a hole in the ground or moving the car or anything like that. All she can do is sit on her ass and cry and slobber all over Mark's shirtfront and—"

"I said, cut it!" David repeated angrily, and Jeff, glancing over at her in surprise, said, "What's got into you, Bets? You're sure in a shitty mood. None of us are looking forward to this part, but it's got to be done, and you said yourself it's good not having Sue along."

"Okay, now," Mark said, cutting off the conversation with a gesture of his hand, "we're almost to the clearing. There ahead—right around the bend." He strained forward in the seat. "There's the car. You did bring the key, Jeff?"

"Sure. I wouldn't come without *that*."

"Okay, pull up next to it here and let's get going. We don't have a whole lot of time if we want to hit the five o'clock traffic. You've got the shovel?"

"In the trunk."

"Just one?"

"It's all I could find," Jeff said. "We'll have to take turns with it."

"Well, get it and follow along behind us, then. Dave and I'll go ahead and check the place over for the best spot for digging."

When they reached the waterfall, Betsy gave a little gasp and covered her face with her hands. "Oh, God—there are *flies* on him!"

"What did you expect?" Mark said, amused. "He doesn't know the difference."

"Ugh—it's grotesque. I'm going downstream and sit and watch the water." She wrinkled her nose in disgust. "I've never seen a dead person before except at a funeral."

"This *is* a sort of funeral," Mark said. "Dave, where do you think? Right by the bank over there?"

"I guess so," David said, swallowing hard.

"There aren't many rocks there, which will make it easier. Here comes Jeff. You want to start us off, Jeff boy? You're the tower of strength among us. How about breaking ground there by the stream?"

"Good enough, but I'm damned if I'm doing the whole thing." Jeff stuck the corner of the shovel into the earth and turned up a lump of soil. "I wish I had a spade. A pointed tip would sure make things easier."

"Well, we don't have one, so dig in with what you've got. Dave, give me a hand and let's roll the guy over. There's no sense burying a wallet full of cash along with him."

"Is that it, in the hip pocket?" David asked grimly.

"Yeah, here it is. A real beat-up old thing, isn't it? Hell, there's only a couple of bucks and a blank check and some credit cards. Too bad we can't use those.

Hey—" Mark's face brightened "—that gives me a great idea! There's a guy I know up in Denver where I used to live who can really copy a signature. I mean, once when I was pretty young I got him to write a check and sign my dad's name to it, and the two of us had spending money for a month before the bank statement came in and my old man caught on to what had happened. This guy and I have kept in touch, and I bet if I sent him Mr. G.'s credit cards he wouldn't say no to buying himself a few nice things with them. Then, the first of the month, in will come the bills to Mrs. G. with her husband's signature right there big as life, charging things from stores in Colorado. Wouldn't that freak out everybody?"

"Man, you're a genius." Jeff was beginning to breathe hard as he dug. "Say, I'm starting to feel like one of the grave-diggers in *Hamlet*. 'Alas, poor Griffin, I knew him, Horatio.' Somebody else take a turn."

"You dig awhile, Dave," Mark said. "Let's see, when I send the credit cards I'd better send along the driver's license for identification. Let me check what else is in here. A library card—we don't need that. Here's a picture of some dame, maybe his wife. Not bad looking. I wonder what she saw in Mr. G.?"

"Don't ask me," Jeff said. "You think Betsy's okay?"

"Sure. She's a tough chick. Where'd she go, anyway?"

"She's down there at the place where we had the picnic."

"Maybe you'd better go talk to her," Mark said. "We can't have her getting cute on us. We're going to need her to drive down one of the cars."

Jeff walked downstream to where Betsy sat, dipping her hand in the water. She lifted her arm and held it suspended, letting the shinning silver droplets fall back into the stream.

"You playing at being Ophelia?" Jeff asked.

"Don't joke, Jeff. This is just *sickening*. I'm sitting here trying not to throw up."

"It didn't bother you this way before," Jeff said.

"That was before I saw him. It was all like a story then, just something David made up and we all went along with. It was even sort of exciting. I didn't picture him like that, all stiff and his eyes wide open and *flies*. I don't see why Sue got out of coming up here and I had to."

"Mark explained," Jeff said. "You want Sue to crack and blab on us?"

"I don't think that's the real reason. You saw how she was with Mark last night, hanging on to him and crying and being all helpless, and the way he fussed over her—'Susie, it's all right, baby; it's all right, sweetie.' "

"It worked, didn't it? He got her simmered down. What's it to you, anyway? Mark's not your private property."

"I don't like to see him lowering himself that way. It's degrading."

"That's a weird thing to say." Jeff gave her an odd look. "Whose girl friend are you anyway, Mark's or mine?"

"That's a stupid question."

"So, I'm stupid. Or maybe I'm just beginning to get over being stupid." There was a strange, flat note to his voice. "How long has it been since we've been out anywhere without Mark? Weeks? Months, maybe? How about last week when I wanted to see that motorcycle flick at the drive-in, and Mark had already seen it, and you said you didn't want to go and we should pick something else to do so Mark could be in on it?"

"He's your best friend, isn't he? I didn't want him to feel left out."

"The way you're acting, you'd think he was *your* best friend."

"Jeffrey Garrett, you're talking like some sort of jealous—"

"Hey, Jeff!" Mark's voice rang down to them, faint against the sound of the rushing water. "Come here and take over the digging, will you? Dave's all in."

"You'd better pull yourself together," Jeff said gruffly to Betsy, "because you're going to be driving one of the cars." He turned on his heel and strode back upstream to where David stood, leaning on the shovel, staring down morosely into the shallow pit that was the result of their efforts.

"You didn't make much headway," Jeff told him irritably.

"I did my best. My arms are about to fall off."

"Time's running out on us, Jeff," Mark said. "You'll have to finish this up. Another foot or so should do it, I think."

"It better," Jeff growled, "because I'm not taking it down any farther."

He took the shovel from David's hands and began to plunge it into the earth with great, ferocious stabs.

"That's a boy," Mark said. "At this rate we'll have it done in no time." He stood watching, his hands in his pockets. Suddenly he smiled. "We should have brought along a radio."

"Why's that?"

"A little music makes work go faster. Besides, there's always music at funerals. We could pick out some good songs for this one. 'Down by the Old Mill

Stream' would be appropriate, or that Scottish thing, 'Where, oh, where, has my highland laddie gone?' "

"Some joke," Jeff muttered. But a moment later he smiled slightly also. "Yeah, and The Grateful Dead could lead the singing."

"Good one. Then just 'specially for Betsy they'd do 'Brush away the blue-tail fly.' "

Mark was hyper, running on a frequency above all of them. His eyes were shining so that their gray glittered like silver. He rocked back and forth from his toes to his heels, anticipating each shovelful of dirt as it was lifted from the grave.

"That should do it," he said after a time. "It would be better if it were deeper, but there just isn't time for that. Let's lower in the body. Dave, what are you doing there?"

"Just—just—" David was kneeling beside the dead man. He glanced up, almost guiltily. "I thought—his eyes—ought to be closed."

"That's a nice gesture." Mark turned to Jeff. "Go call Betsy up here. We can't let her miss the last chapter."

"She's pretty upset, Mark. I think we ought to let her be."

"Okay, if you say so. You know her better than I do. What's that you're doing now, Dave?"

David had taken off his Windbreaker and laid it over the face of the man on the ground.

"This will keep the dirt off him."

"He won't know the difference."

"*I* will though," David said stiffly. "I don't want the dirt to be right on his face."

"Suit yourself. It's your jacket. Are we ready? Jeff, get a grip under his shoulders. Dave, get his feet."

"I don't want to," David said. "You do it."

"It's almost over, boy!"

"I said, you do it."

David turned abruptly and started back along the path toward the clearing. The thin, golden rays of the late afternoon sun fell on his back and shoulders, but the air had already grown cool enough to make him shiver. The hands at his sides were gripped into fists, fingernails biting into the palms. He could still feel the shape of the shovel handle as his fingers curled around it.

"It has to be done," Mark had said, and it was true, and "He doesn't know the difference," and that was true also. If the words the Reverend Chandler spoke from the pulpit were correct the body they had come to bury was no more than the deserted shell of the man. Somewhere, even now, the soul of Brian Griffin soared high and free into eternal glory, the anguish of his last hours on earth of no more significance in retrospect than the discomfort of his birth.

We should have said a prayer, David thought, and since he could not bring himself to turn and go back, he began to recite one, drawing comfort from the familiarity of the words that he had murmured nightly since babyhood.

"Our Father—which art in heaven—hallowed be Thy name—"

He reached the end of the path and stepped out into the clearing where the two cars stood side by side. He started first for Jeff's car and then, on impulse, opened instead the door of the Chevrolet and climbed in behind the steering wheel. In times past he had sometimes amused himself by contemplating how cars often seemed extensions of the people who owned them. There was Jeff's car, large and loud and flashy, and David's mother's, compact, economical and serviceable. Betsy's mother's Volkswagen was small and fitful, a nervous little automobile, painted bright yellow.

Now, in Brian Griffin's car, he closed his eyes and tried to feel the presence of the man who had driven it, hoping for one last image of warmth and life. It did not come. The car was as cold and devoid of personality as the thing in the grave by the waterfall.

"We didn't do it," David whispered. "It was an accident, something that would have happened anyway. We weren't responsible." He kept whispering it over and over, and somehow he worked it into the prayer so that the two became one—"forgive us our trespasses—we didn't do it—deliver us from evil—it was an accident." He kept his eyes closed, mouthing the words in a desperate attempt to project them into space. "For Thine is the kingdom—we were not responsible. Please, please, believe me, it would have happened anyhow."

He heard their voices as they came back along the path, and opened his eyes and saw them approaching. Mark was in the lead, a strange Mark, no longer the cool, sullen, self-contained young man with the sleepy eyes, but a vivacious, sparkling Mark, talking and talking.

Who is that person? David asked himself as he watched the boy come striding toward him across the clearing. I have never seen that person before. It was as though the life that had left Mr. Griffin had spilled over into Mark Kinney, and he was filled suddenly with an uncontainable double portion. Behind him, Jeff seemed almost stolid, and Betsy was tight-faced and expressionless.

"There you are," Mark said as he reached the car. "What did you run off for, boy? Well, it's over and done now, and all that's left is the bit with the car.

Bets, you drive down Griffin's and Jeff and I will follow along and pick you up at the north end of the
airport parking lot."

"Why me?" Betsy asked. "I've never driven that
car."

"You won't have any trouble with it. It drives fine.
If I could, I'd keep it for myself, but that's not worth
the risk. You drive it because you're a girl and nobody's going to expect a girl to be driving around in
Mr. G.'s car. Dave, you go along with her. When you
reach the airport, pull into the lower lot where they
have the long-term parking. Take a handkerchief and
wipe your prints off the steering wheel and anything
else you may have handled. Leave the car unlocked
and the key in the ignition."

"Why should they leave the key?" Jeff asked.
"Somebody might rip it off."

"That's the whole idea," Mark said with a grin.
"Can you think of a better way to get rid of a car than
to have somebody steal it?"

"If the guy who takes it gets picked up with it—"

"That's his problem, not ours."

"Say, that's okay." Jeff regarded Mark with grudg-
ing respect. "You've really thought out everything."

"The thing that bothers me is, what if I get
stopped?" Betsy protested. "The police are bound to
be looking for the car by this time. What do I say if
somebody spots us?"

"Nobody will if you do your job right," Mark told
her. "Drive slowly and carefully and don't do anything
to draw attention. Join the line of cars coming out of
the factories. Dave will be with you to keep his eye
peeled for cops. He'll spot them before they spot you,
and if you see one, pull into the first driveway you see
as though you lived there, and wait till he passes."

"All right," Betsy agreed nervously.

David slid over on the seat and let her in behind the wheel. They had little to say to each other. Betsy started the engine, and they drove back down to the highway and followed the line of the mountain range north and west until it intersected with Coors Road. There, as Mark had predicted, they were immediately caught up in a stream of traffic that swept them anonymously past the outer edges of town.

They reached the airport and pulled into the lot, with Betsy leaning out of the open car window to take the ticket projected from the dispenser at the gate.

"Where shall I park? Does it matter?"

"I can't think why. Any space should do." Suddenly David caught his breath. "Our luck's run out on us. There's a police car behind us."

"Right here in the lot!" Betsy glanced in the rear-view mirror and her face went ashen, the freckles standing out like bright blobs of paint. "He followed us in! Or—did he? Maybe he's just here to park like anyone else while he goes into the terminal for something. What shall I do?"

"You don't have a choice. Just park somewhere. If you turn around now and drive out again it will catch his attention for sure."

"Here's a space," Betsy said. "Is he still behind us?"

"No, he's pulling on past. I think you're right, he's going to park."

"Oh, thank heaven!" She pulled the car carefully into the empty parking place and turned off the ignition. "Let's get out and go!"

"First we've got to get rid of our fingerprints."

"That will take forever!"

"No it won't. We haven't touched much. Don't get panicky." David ran his handkerchief swiftly around the circle of the steering wheel and along the window ledges. Then he wiped off the key. "Anything else?"

"No, nothing. Let's get going."

Using the handkerchief as a shield between their hands and the metal handles of the doors, they opened the doors and got out of the car. The police car was parked two rows over and several spaces to the north. The driver had just climbed out and was crossing the lot in the direction of the airport.

"We'll have to walk right by him," Betsy whispered.

"That's okay," David told her. "If he recognized the car he'd have done something by now. He's just another guy stopping to pick up reservations or meet somebody." He took her arm. "Walk slowly, keep your eyes on my face, and keep talking. He won't even notice us."

"What can I talk about? My mind's gone blank."

"About school. About the game the other night. It doesn't matter, just jabber. And for Christ sake, smile!"

Amazingly, she did—the bright, full, cheerleader smile that was her trademark. It lit up her face as though she had pressed a light switch.

"It was the most exciting game!" she said breathlessly. "You just can't imagine how close it was! Right up until the last two minutes we were neck and neck. Then, Jeff got the ball, and he went charging down the floor and—"

"'Afternoon, Miss Cline," the policeman said pleasantly as he passed them.

THIRTEEN

The story was on the six o'clock news, and Mr. McConnell brought it up at dinner.

"On television this evening they were telling about a Del Norte teacher who's been reported missing."

"Missing?" Mrs. McConnell repeated. "Missing, how? Do you mean he's simply disappeared?"

"That's about the size of it. He taught his classes yesterday and then never was seen again. His name's Brian Griffin. Sue, don't you have a class with him?"

"Yes," Susan said faintly. "English, first period."

"They gave his description—forty-one years old, medium height and weight, dark hair, a mustache. The car he drives is missing also, a dark green Chevy."

"I wish my teachers would disappear," Craig said enviously. "Sue gets all the luck."

"Don't joke about something like this, Craig," his mother said. "Think how you would feel if it were Dad. Personally, I can't imagine anything more horrible than to have something like this occur to someone in your family. The waiting, the uncertainty, all the terrible possibilities that would float through your mind would be enough to drive the soundest person totally insane."

"He's married too," Mr. McConnell said. "They said his wife is offering a thousand-dollar reward for any information leading to his location."

"That's a lot of money," Francis said. "Boy, I sure wish I knew where he was. Think, Mel—a thousand dollars! We'd be rich!"

"What would you do with it?" Melvynne asked. "I'd buy models. And a new ten-speed."

"I'd buy Bruce Rogoff's drum set," Craig said. "You know those neat drums his folks bought him for his birthday? Well, he's tired of them. He wants a sax instead."

"Imagine!" Mrs. McConnell exclaimed. "Those expensive drums!" And they were off on another subject with Brian Griffin forgotten.

I am not going to think about him, Susan told herself desperately. I will make my mind go on to other things.

So she tried her best to contribute to the dinner-table conversation and found herself noticing small things that she had never appreciated before—the kindness behind her father's teasing; the warmth in her mother's smile; the endearing earnestness with which the twins cut their meat, sawing each slice into careful squares and then shoveling three or four of them into their mouths at once; the bones and angles of Craig's face, emerging suddenly from the soft roundness of childhood.

I love them so much, Susan thought. How could I ever have imagined that I didn't?

And with the thought came a sense of loss as though she had moved a million miles beyond this family and were seeing them in memory, reaching back toward them yet unable to touch them.

I am not Susan any longer, she thought. I am not the person they know as their daughter and their sister. I am a stranger who has lived through things they could not even imagine and who has changed into someone foreign to them all. They look at me and call me "Sue," and I speak back to them, and they never guess how far away from them I am and how much I miss them.

When dinner was over Susan cleared the table and helped Craig load the dishwasher. The twins, whose job it was to wash the pans, stood at the sink and fought over who would do the broiler, and Mr. McConnell went into the den and turned on the television. Mrs. McConnell plugged in the electric coffee maker and got out two cups.

"Would you like some tonight, Sue?"

"No, thank you," Susan said.

The doorbell rang.

"You might as well get it, honey," her mother said. "It will probably be David."

"She can't go out till she's done her part of the kitchen!" Craig objected. "She got out of it last night because she was sick, but it's not fair two nights in a row."

"I'm not going anywhere," Susan told him. "I don't feel like going out."

"Then what's he coming over for?"

But it was not David who stood at the door when Susan went to open it, but a middle-aged woman in a brown car coat.

"I'm looking for Susan McConnell," she said. "Is this the right house?"

"Yes," Susan said, bewildered.

"I'm Mrs. Griffin."

For a moment Susan could not bring herself to move. She stood frozen, staring into the unfamiliar face.

"Who is it, Sue?" her mother called from the kitchen.

When Susan did not answer, Mrs. McConnell came into the hallway.

"Hello. Can I help you?"

"I'm Mrs. Griffin," the woman said again. "Kathy Griffin. I'd like to talk with Susan."

"Mrs. Griffin? The wife of Sue's teacher?" Mrs. McConnell came quickly over to her. "Where are your manners, Sue? Can't you invite your guest inside? Please come in, Mrs. Griffin. We just heard the distressing news about your husband and are so concerned. Is there anything new since the report on the evening news?"

"No, nothing," the woman said.

She stepped through the door into the hallway, and Susan saw that her first impression had been incorrect and Kathy Griffin was no older than her late twenties. It was the strained look of her face that had made her appear older.

"Come, sit down," Susan's mother said. "Let me take your coat. Can I get you some coffee? My husband and I were just going to have some."

"No, thank you." Under the coat the woman was wearing navy-blue slacks and a pink maternity blouse with a white collar. She looked very tired. "I just wanted to talk with your daughter a few minutes. According to the police, she was the last person to see my husband yesterday, and she told them some things that I just can't accept."

"Sue was the last to see him?" Mrs. McConnell

turned to Susan in surprise. "You didn't tell us that."

"Didn't I?" Susan said. "I thought I did."

"Of course you didn't." Her mother gestured the other woman toward a chair. "Please, sit down. I'm sure Sue wants to help in any way she can. Let me get my husband; he'll want to help too, if possible. We all do." She raised her voice. "Ed? Come out here, dear. Mr. Griffin's wife is here to talk with Sue."

Mr. McConnell came in from the den, and introductions were made, and the twins and Craig came in, bright faced and curious, and were also introduced and were then sent back to the kitchen. I cannot go through with this, Susan thought, and yet somehow she found herself seated on the sofa between her parents with Mrs. Griffin directly across from her, and she was saying, "Yes, I had a conference with him after school. I did see him then."

"What did you talk about?" Kathy Griffin asked her. "Your 'Song for Ophelia'?"

The question was so far from what she had expected that Susan stopped, disconcerted. "Why, yes—he did mention that. How did you know?"

"He told me about it at breakfast. He said your song was an exceptionally good one, that you were a sensitive young writer."

"He did?"

"What song?" Mrs. McConnell asked. "I'm afraid you've left us behind here. Did you write a song, Sue?"

"Not with music," Susan said. "It was more of a poem. It was to be the last song Ophelia sang before her death. We all had to do it. It was an assignment."

"Brian isn't an easy teacher," Kathy Griffin said. "He's demanding of his students—too demanding, I sometimes think. He feels he has such a short time with them, he wants to bring them just as far as he can before they're out of his hands. He's a dedicated teacher, and he gets very excited about his better students. He considers Susan one of his 'good ones.' "

"That's a fine compliment," Mr. McConnell said. "I'm sure it must mean a lot to Sue to hear that."

"It's because of that—because she has been special to him—I couldn't believe—" She turned her gaze from the senior McConnells to Susan herself, directing the question to her. "Why did you lie to the police about what Brian did when he left school?"

There was a moment of stunned silence.

Then Susan said, "I don't know what you mean."

"Of course you know. You made up several things about that interview. You told the police that Brian was jumpy, that he kept glancing at his watch and hardly paid any attention to what he was talking about. I know that's not true. Brian took his conferences with students very seriously. He made notes ahead of time of the things he wanted to discuss with them. He cared—he cared deeply about such things. He would not have acted the way you said he did."

"He did," Susan said. "He kept looking at his watch."

"What would you say if I told you Brian wasn't wearing a watch?"

"He was," Susan said. "He always wore a watch." She paused. "Didn't he?"

"Usually, yes. But day before yesterday it broke. The crystal fell out. It's at home on his bureau right now, waiting for me to take it to be repaired."

Oh, dear God, Susan thought. Panic began to rise within her, pushing its way up from her stomach into her throat with a cold, sour pressure. She swallowed hard.

"Maybe he borrowed a watch from somebody, just for the day."

"Why would he do that? There are clocks all over the school. Every room has one. Besides, Brian never borrows things. He doesn't believe in it. 'Neither a borrower nor a lender be,' he says. He says it *all* the time. Do you know what that's from?"

"*Hamlet*." She could have told her the act, the scene, the line.

"Why did you make that up about the watch, Susan?"

"I didn't," Susan said. "I thought he was wearing one. He acted as though he were. He kept—he kept—" She groped for words. "He kept looking—at his wrist—the way somebody does who is used to wearing a watch and is concerned about what time it is. I mean, people like that, even if they're not wearing their watches, they're so in the habit of looking at the wrists, they keep on doing it."

"That sounds reasonable," Mr. McConnell said quietly. "What I'd like to know, Mrs. Griffin, is why is it so important that your husband was or wasn't wearing a watch during his conference with our daughter? It seems like a very insignificant thing."

"It might be," Kathy Griffin said, "except that it points up the fact that Susan isn't telling the whole and complete truth. There's no reason for her to say that Brian looked at his watch if he didn't. Why would someone invent such a statement? There has to be a reason. Why did you say it, Susan?"

"Because I thought it was true."

"Why did you say there was a woman waiting for Brian out in his car?"

"Because there was."

"No, there wasn't. That's another lie—a total lie!"

Kathy's eyes were blazing. In an instant the pale, drawn face was alive with anger. "You made that up! Why?"

"I didn't make anything up," Susan said. "There was a woman. Young. Blond. Very pretty. She was sitting in the front seat—not in the driver's seat, in the other one."

"How did you come to see this woman, Sue?" her father asked.

"Mr. Griffin and I were talking, and we walked out together into the parking lot. We stood by his car and talked a little longer, and then I turned and started home. And then—" Frantically she fished backward in her mind for Mark's words. "And then—something about the way he'd been acting made me look back, and he was getting into his car. And the woman was there!"

"You hadn't seen her the whole time you were standing beside the car talking to Brian?" Kathy Griffin asked.

"No. I wasn't looking inside the car. I didn't notice."

"And with this woman—this 'dolly'—sitting there waiting for him, Brian still had you walk with him to the lot, had you stand right there next to the car and continue the conversation you were having inside, the conversation he had hardly paid any attention to because he was so busy looking at the watch he wasn't wearing?"

"Yes," Susan said. "Yes, he did."

"Could you describe this woman in more detail?"

"I already said she was blond and young."

"What was she wearing?"

"A green blouse," Susan said desperately. "And a matching sweater. And pants—brown pants."

"You could see the pants even though she was seated inside the car?"

"When Mr. Griffin opened the car door to get in on the driver's side, I could see across."

"On your way across the parking lot, glancing back over your shoulder, you could see into the car and across the seat and notice and remember every detail of this strange woman's clothing?"

"Mrs. Griffin," Susan's father said, "if Sue says she saw this woman, then she saw her. There is no reason for her to tell you this if it isn't true."

"That's the whole point," Kathy Griffin said. "There *must* be a reason. There has to be one for Susan to have told the police all these things. Unless she's some sort of compulsive liar and doesn't know the difference between truth and falsehoods, unless she lies all the time about everything and it's just part of her makeup—"

"That's ridiculous!" Mrs. McConnell said. There was a note of anger in her normally gentle voice. "Susan does not lie."

"How can you be so certain about that?"

"Because she's our daughter," Mrs. McConnell said. "We have lived with Sue for sixteen years and we *know* her. When you know and love somebody you're aware of her faults as well as her good points, and if Susan were inclined to fabricate stories we would certainly have discovered it by now."

"I feel the same way exactly about my husband," Kathy Griffin said. "I *know* him, and he did *not* leave the school with some beautiful woman and forget to come home. Something else happened to Brian, something I can't even begin to imagine, but Susan can. Susan knows what it is, or she wouldn't be trying so hard to mislead us."

"Are you implying that our daughter did something to your husband?" Mr. McConnell asked incredulously.

"Not by herself. Or maybe not at all. Maybe she just knows something about someone else who did. Maybe she *saw* something."

"Did you see something, Sue?" her father asked.

"No, of course not! I didn't see anything I haven't already told you about!" Susan felt herself growing close to hysteria. "I saw a woman—a blond woman—in Mr. Griffin's car. I didn't see anything else or anybody else—just that."

"If my daughter says—" Mr. McConnell began.

The doorbell rang. There was the sound of footsteps, of the door opening, and then Craig's voice, "Oh, hi. Sue, it's David!"

"It is?" Susan half rose, then forced herself to sink back again. She struggled to keep the relief that surged through her from flooding her voice. "Dave? I'm here—here in the living room!"

"This is David Ruggles, a friend of Sue's." Mrs. McConnell made automatic introductions. "Dave, this is Mrs. Griffin. Oh—I didn't see—you have a friend with you?"

"Mark Kinney," David said.

Thank God! Susan could have thrown her arms around both of them in gratitude for their interruption of the interview. She could see David stiffen slightly as he realized who the woman in the armchair was, but he held himself in check, smiling and extending his hand.

"I'm glad to meet you, ma'am."

Mark did not show recognition of any kind. His face was bland and expressionless as he acknowledged the introduction with a nod.

"I'm sorry," David said. "I didn't know you had company. Mark and I were just out riding around, and we thought maybe Sue would like to get a Coke or something."

"I'd love to," Susan said. Anywhere, anything, to leave this room and the pressure of the confrontation. She was on her feet in an instant.

Her mother reached out quickly and laid a restraining hand on her arm.

"Mrs. Griffin may have more things to ask you, dear."

"I don't have anything more," Kathy Griffin said quietly. "I know Susan's eager to go out with her friends. Are you boys in my husband's class also?"

"Yes," David said.

"What was your name—Ruggles? Yes, of course, Brian mentioned you only yesterday. Your papers blew away on your way to class. Is that right?"

"Yes," David said again, startled. "He told you about that?"

"Brian talks a lot about his students. Everything that happens in connection with his teaching is important to him. And, you—" She turned to Mark, frowning slightly in concentration. "Mark Kinney. That name rings a bell too, though I haven't heard it so recently. There was something last year—oh, I remember. You're the boy who copied a term paper from the university."

"I'm afraid so, Mrs. Griffin." Mark dropped his eyes. "I was going through sort of a problem time in my life last year, and I made some mistakes I've been sorry for. I was lucky to have somebody like your husband there to help me get straightened out."

"There was a girl who got the paper for you. She was a university student, wasn't she?"

"I guess she must have been," Mark said.

"Her name—"

"I don't remember. I hardly knew her. Like I said, that was a kind of freaked-out time for me. I've put it behind me."

"I'm glad." Placing her hands on the arms of the chair, Kathy Griffin hoisted herself laboriously to her feet. "I'll think about it awhile. I'll remember the girl's name."

Susan's parents rose too. Mrs. McConnell regarded the younger woman with concern.

"I'm sorry Susan couldn't have been of more help to you, Mrs. Griffin. I know how upset and worried you must be. If we can help you in any way—"

"Thank you." Kathy Griffin's eyes were not on her, but on Susan. "I think Susan *can* be of more help, if she wants to be. Perhaps she will recall something later and want to contact me."

"If she does, I'm sure she'll call you at once," Mr. McConnell said. "Won't you, Sue?"

"Of course," Susan said.

FOURTEEN

Davy's been up to something," Irma Ruggles said.

Her daughter-in-law paused, her arms piled high with bed sheets, her face reflecting a mixture of amusement and exasperation.

"What is it with you and David these days, Mother Ruggles? The two of you are at each other over everything. Yesterday morning at breakfast you were practically accusing him of trying to poison you."

"No, I mean it. Davy's been up to something he doesn't want us to know about."

"Like what?"

Irma paused for effect and then spoke slowly with each word carefully enunciated.

"Davy's been seeing his daddy."

There was a moment of silence. Then David's mother said quietly, "You know that's totally impossible. David's father has been gone fourteen years."

"That doesn't mean he can't come back again."

"If he were going to do that, it would have been a long time ago."

"He picked his time to go and he can pick his time to come back. There's no rule that says when." The gray-haired woman began to rock slowly back and forth in her chair. "I've always known he'd be back someday. I've always known that before I died I'd see my boy again."

"What is it that makes you think he's back in town?" her daughter-in-law asked her.

"Well, to start with, there's the way Davy's acting. He's gone all the time, off someplace, seeing somebody."

"David's been out more than usual, yes, but he tells us where he goes. Last weekend he went on a picnic in the mountains. For the past couple of nights he's been seeing that girl he likes, that Susan."

"What about yesterday afternoon when he never came home from school at all? You got home from work, and he still wasn't here."

"That was thoughtless of him, and I talked to him about it. He was out riding around with the Kinney boy and some friends of his and lost track of time. It's irritating, Mother, but boys are like that, and David is seventeen, after all."

"Then the day before—the day he made the Jell-O—"

"You're not back on that again!" The amusement was gone. The exasperation had won. She came into the room and set the pile of sheets down on the stripped mattress of the bed.

"You and David had that all out yesterday morning. He was here with you all Thursday afternoon. It's not his fault that you fell asleep and don't remember."

"He wasn't here. He went out."

"What makes you keep saying that?"

"He didn't watch the game show. He told me the

girl with the curly hair won again, remember? He said she won a mixer."

"Of course, I remember."

"Well, she didn't win. Not a mixer, not anything. I tuned in on the show yesterday, and if that girl had won she'd have been back again trying for more prizes. She lost, and there was a black girl in purple pants instead."

"Mother, honestly!"

"He wasn't here. He didn't see it," the old woman insisted. "He was out somewhere that afternoon, and I know where. He was with his daddy. His daddy's right here in town, and he's got hold of Davy, and he's seeing him."

"Look, Mother," the younger Mrs. Ruggles said patiently, "Big David went away because he didn't want the responsibility of a family. He wanted to be a free spirit, floating where he would, without a wife and a child and a sick mother dragging him down. We're all still here, the three of us. Why would he suddenly decide to come back now?"

"Men change."

"Some of them, maybe. But if he has changed—suddenly, after this long a time—then why would he be hiding out, contacting David on the sly? Why wouldn't he come over here and knock on the door and walk right in?"

"You don't want him back," Irma Ruggles challenged. "You don't want to believe he's here, because you don't want him. You never wanted him."

"That's not true. You know that when David left us, I felt like the whole world had caved in. For years I waited and hoped. Every time the phone rang my heart would drop into my stomach, I was so sure it would be his voice on the other end. Every time I came home from work and the mail was lying on the floor under the slot in the door, I held my breath when I bent down to pick it up, thinking maybe—maybe—there will be something from David."

"That was the way you were supposed to act. You always act the way you're supposed to."

"What are you saying?"

"I'm saying some women aren't made to be wives," Irma Ruggles said. "They've got to run the whole show themselves. I know you felt bad there in the beginning, after my boy run off, and I felt real sorry for you, but you came around fast. 'Poor, brave girl, look how wonderful she is,' everybody said, and you liked that. You liked being wonderful."

"I'm sorry," her daughter-in-law said in a low, tight voice, "but I'm not going to listen to any more of this. You're not well, Mother Ruggles. You're not thinking straight. You're an old lady—"

"Being old doesn't mean you can't see things clear. I see things fine. I see more than you do, all wrapped up like you are in being busy. I see Davy acting funny, and I know—I know."

"I've got to go out for a while," the younger woman said, leaning to pick up the sheets once more. "You know Saturday's the only day I have to get to the Laundromat."

"Where's Davy?"

"He went over to one of his friends' house for a while, but he promised he'd be back by five. If he's home before I am, tell him to put some potatoes in to bake. We'll eat early tonight."

"You don't believe it, what I've been telling you?"

"No, Mother Ruggles."

"Well, I've got proof," the old woman said. "Real proof." She slipped her hand into the pocket of her

robe, groped for a moment, and then smiled with satisfaction as her fingers closed upon a small, hard object.

"I've got proof," she said. "I got it out of Davy's
room this morning. Davy's been seeing his daddy, and
I've got proof!"

But there was no longer anyone to listen. In the
room beyond, the front door of the house opened and
closed.

Detective Baca held the plastic vial carefully with
his handkerchief and turned it so that he could exam-
ine the label.

"Now, where exactly did you say you found this?"

"Up in the mountains at a place I like to go sometimes," the girl told him. "My fiancé and I went up
there to have a picnic."

"It was lying by the edge of the stream," the young
man said. "I wouldn't even have noticed it, but Lana
said, 'How funny. Somebody's been up here.' She
picked it up and read the name and said she knows
the guy the label was made out to."

"You know Brian Griffin personally?" Jim Baca
asked the girl.

"Well, not exactly. I've never actually met him, but
a friend of mine took a class from him last year and
had some—problems. I was—sort of —involved in the
situation, and I remembered the name. Then last
night it was on TV about his being missing, and it was
in the paper this morning."

"It's a comparatively new prescription," the detective remarked. "It's dated last month. And the label
looks pretty clean for having been lying outside. Why
were you so surprised to find it where you did?"

"It's not a public picnic area," the girl said. "It's
way back from the road, and the only way you can get

there is to go down a little path that's hidden by some bushes. I just didn't think anybody knew about the place."

"How did *you* know about it?"

"I came onto it about a year ago. I was with a guy— a boy I used to date—and we were hiking, and we came through the woods and all of a sudden, there was this waterfall. It was really pretty, and we went back a few times after that." She glanced over at the boy beside her. "Today—well, I wanted to show it to Chris."

"Lana and I go to school in Portales," the boy volunteered. "We're here over spring break, staying with her folks. They're nice people and all; it's just that it can get sort of heavy—you know?—not ever being alone together. So, Lana said she knew this private place, and—well—we just thought we'd go there."

"I guess, maybe, it was silly, bringing this down to the police station," the girl said, half apologetically. "Chris thought it was. I mean, it's just a little bottle. It doesn't even have anything in it."

"It wasn't silly at all," Jim Baca told her. "It may or may not turn out to be important, but it certainly wasn't 'silly.' Now, what about the rest of the area? Was there anything else lying around up there? Sandwich wrappers, beer cans, anything like that? Something to indicate that people had been there partying?"

"No," the girl said. "But there was another strange thing. There's this big patch of ground with the earth turned up, like people were digging for something."

"Well, it's about time you got here," Mark said shortly. "Where's Jeff?"

"He'll be late," Betsy said, sliding into the booth across from him. "He had practice."

"Practice, for Christ sake! He doesn't think this is important enough to cut practice for?"

"You told us all to keep on doing the things we usually do," David reminded him. "You said if we didn't it would start people wondering."

"Betsy, here, has already started them wondering, if what you told me last night is right." Mark's face was dark with fury.

"What do you mean?" Susan asked in a whisper. "What's Betsy done?"

"She got herself a speeding ticket."

"What's so awful about that?" Betsy asked blankly. "Lots of people get tickets."

"You never even told us!"

Betsy glanced wide-eyed from Mark's face, to David's, and back again.

"I didn't think it was important."

"Not important!" Mark said hoarsely. "It explodes the whole darned alibi! How could you be home entertaining Jeff and me, when you're out getting a speeding ticket a block away from the school?"

"Hey—cool it," David said in a low voice. "Maria's coming for our order."

"Hi there, gang!" The pert, dark-eyed waitress greeted them pleasantly. "How are our most regular customers this afternoon? What can I get you?"

"What do you want, Sue?" David asked her.

"Nothing. I'm not hungry."

"Cokes for everybody," Mark said.

"Large or small?"

"It doesn't matter. Small's fine." He pressed his lips together tightly until the girl had moved away from the table, and then leaned forward, letting his breath out in a soft hiss. "Okay, Bets, now give us the story. How much does this cop know about you?"

"Nothing," Betsy said nervously. "Honestly, Mark, it was just such a little thing I never even thought about it afterward. I was driving over to the school, and I was afraid I'd be late, and I guess I gave it a little more gas than I should have."

"I didn't ask you how it happened, I asked what the guy knows about you. How much did you talk to him?"

"Hardly at all. Just about the ticket."

"You tried to talk him out of it?"

"Well, sure. I mean, after all, my father *is* a County Commissioner."

"And you told him that? 'My daddy's Harold Cline—he's on the County Commission—you don't dare ticket me'? You actually sat there, feeding him that sort of information?"

Betsy's face was her answer.

"Christ, no wonder he remembered you," Mark said savagely. "You rubbed that name right into his mind with a piece of sandpaper. So the next day he sees you and Dave in the airport parking lot, and he comes right out with it. 'Here's Miss Cline again.' "

"He didn't say that," Betsy said. "He said, 'Good afternoon,' or something like that. It wasn't any big deal."

"But he *saw* you, and he *knew* you. He saw you get out of Griffin's car, Dave says. In fact, he got a good long look at the car. He followed you right into the parking lot. Right?"

"That's right," David said, "but I don't think he really noticed much. If he'd recognized the car as one on the wanted list, he'd have reacted right then. He'd have asked us for the registration or something."

"He may not have recognized it right off," Mark said, "but you can be darned sure he's got it wedged into some corner of his brain, just the way he wedged in Betsy's name. All it'll take now is for one of his superiors to read out the description during briefing, and out it'll come. 'Hey,' he'll say, 'I've seen a car like that. It's down at the airport.' "

"What can we do?" Susan asked. "Go down and move it?"

"We'll have to. There's no time now to sit around and wait for some dude to rip it off. But where can we stow it? Christ, Betsy, I'd like to strangle you."

"I'm sorry," Betsy said contritely. "I didn't mean to make problems."

"So you didn't mean to; a lot of good that does us! Well, put your mind to it and see what you can come up with. We've got to find a safe place to stow that car, and we've got to do it now."

"We could paint it and maybe sell it," Susan said.

"Without the title? You must be nuts."

"What about dumping it out at one of the Indian pueblos?" David suggested. "You know, they're private land. The police can't go poking around on them without special permission from their governors. A car could sit there for a long time without being reported."

"Which pueblo? The closest is Sandia, and that's too small. The Indians there know every car that comes in and out. Zuni's bigger, but who wants to drive a hot car a couple of hundred miles on interstate highways to reach it?"

"I have an idea," Betsy said. "Let's take it out on the mesa and scrap it. I mean, just tear it apart, knock it into pieces, and scatter them."

"With what, a sledgehammer? Should we cut it up into half-inch hunks with a metal saw? How many years do you think that would take us, if we ever did get it done?"

"Well, *you* suggest something," David said. "You're the big idea guy."

"I did think of something—the airport. It would have been perfect too, if Betsy hadn't screwed things up for us. Okay, we're stuck now. The best I can come up with is that we stick it in the Garretts' garage."

"In their garage!" Betsy exclaimed. "Why, that's not hiding it! Jeff's parents will see it right away."

"So they see it. Jeff can tell them he's working on the engine for a friend."

"For how long?" David asked skeptically. "For a couple of days? A week?"

"For as long as it's got to be before we figure out something else. The main thing is, we've got to get that car out of the airport lot and under cover fast. When that cop goes back to the lot to look at it, it's got to be gone."

"Jeff's parents have a two-car garage," Betsy said. "Jeff can park his own car in the driveway. It wouldn't be the first time; he did some work on Greg Dart's car just last month."

"And while he's got it he can spray it with paint," Mark said. "And we can do something about digging up a different license plate. Yeah, this is the best answer. If we get the car looking different we can travel with it. Then maybe we can follow up on Dave's idea and take it out to Zuni."

"How do you know Jeff will agree to this?" Susan asked. "Having it right there in his own garage and everything?"

"He's got to agree. He doesn't have a choice."

"What if his parents recognize it from the description in the paper?"

"They won't," Mark said. "There are lots of green Chevies in the world. Besides, they've got no reason to be suspicious of anything Jeff does. He messes around with cars all the time."

"Here comes Maria with the Cokes," David said. "Oh—and there's Jeff." He raised his hand to catch the attention of the boy who had just come in. Their eyes caught, and Jeff started across the room toward the table.

He reached them just as the waitress was distributing the last of the drinks.

"I was wondering where you were," she said with a smile. "How's my best customer today? Hamburger and fries as usual?"

"No," Jeff said. "Nothing for me."

"Not even a Coke?"

"I said, I don't want anything."

Betsy slid over to make room for him, and Jeff wedged himself in beside her. His face was without its usual ruddy coloring, and his mouth was set strangely.

The others regarded him in silence until Maria had moved out of earshot. Then Mark asked, "What's happened?"

"I heard it on the car radio," Jeff said. "They've found it."

"Then all our worry over where to move it was for nothing," Betsy moaned. "What did they say, Jeff? Was there anything about Dave and me being seen parking it?"

"They didn't find the car," Jeff said hoarsely. "It's the body. They've found Griffin."

"That's impossible," Mark said. "It's some kind of trick. Nobody knows that place but us. There's no way they could have found him."

"They said they did. His wife's identified him. They said his wallet was missing."

"I knew it," Susan whispered. "There's no way we could have gotten away with it."

"They're guessing about the wallet. It stands to reason, nobody'd dump a guy without taking his wallet." Mark's full attention was on Jeff. "Did they say where they found him? Did they mention Dave's Windbreaker?"

"No. It was real brief, just a news flash. They said the wallet was gone and his Stanford ring was missing from his finger."

"Well, that proves it's a trick. We didn't take any ring. They're throwing the whole thing out to see if they can get a reaction. It's a scare thing."

"Do you still want to move the car?" Betsy asked.

"The sooner the better. Jeff will take you to the lot, and you follow him back to his place. We're stashing the Chevy in your garage for a while, Jeff." Mark was all business.

"I don't want it at my place," Jeff objected. "That thing's hot as hell."

"There's no place else. Keep the garage door shut and give it a fast paint job." Mark turned to David. "You ride along with Betsy as a lookout."

"I can't," David said. "I've got to get Sue home and get back to my own place. I told my mom I'd be back by five."

"What a life you lead. It's like punching a time clock." Mark grimaced. "Okay, I'll ride lookout. First I'm going to the men's room and cut up Griffin's credit cards and flush them down the john. And I'm dumping the wallet in the garbage. And, so help me, Bets, if you get stopped for a ticket during this ride, you've had it."

"If you don't think they've really found him, why are you getting rid of everything?" Susan asked in a thin voice.

Mark did not appear to hear her. He got up and left the table.

FIFTEEN

Where are we going?" Susan asked. "This isn't the way to my house."

"We're going by my place first," David told her. "If my mom's back from the laundry, I'll borrow her car and take you home."

"But why your place?" She was half running to keep up with him.

"There's something I've got to get there."

"David, please, slow down. People are staring at us." She caught hold of his arm, forcing him to slacken his pace, trying to get him to turn and look at her. "Please tell me what this is all about. You're not—" The thought struck her suddenly, filling her with a mixture of terror and relief—"You're not going to report it, are you?"

"Report it? You mean, turn us all in?" Now he did look at her, his eyes wide and incredulous. "You've got to be kidding."

"Kidding? About *that*? Do you really think I'd kid about anything now?" She tightened her grip on his arm. "We could drive down to the police station and—just tell them. We could explain how it all happened—how we never meant it—"

"Don't talk that way," David said harshly. "Don't even start thinking like that. It's too late."

"Too late? Why?"

"They'd never believe us. We've waited too long. Maybe you were right in the first place when you wanted to go to your father. If we'd gone in right after it happened we might have been believed. But not now. My God, Sue, we buried him! We dug a hole and put him in the ground. Innocent people wouldn't have done that, would they?"

"We're not innocent, but we're not murderers either. If we confessed, it would be all over."

"It would be over all right, but not in the way you mean it." His voice was flat and expressionless. "The one hope we've got is to keep our mouths shut and cover our tracks as completely as possible. You heard what Mark said about getting rid of the credit cards."

"Mark says it's a trick—that they didn't really find him."

"It isn't a trick."

"Mark says—"

"I don't care what Mark says," David said shortly. "It isn't a trick. They've dug up Griffin and identified him. That part about the ring is right. It wasn't on his finger."

"How do you know?" Susan asked.

"Because I took it off."

"You—what?" She couldn't believe she was hearing him correctly. "You took off his ring—and kept it?"

David nodded.

"How could you do such a thing? *Why* did you do it?"

"I don't know."

"You have to know. You had to be thinking of something. Were you planning to sell it?" The moment she asked the question she longed to snatch it back again. The idea of David Ruggles stealing a ring from a dead man's hand in order to sell it was inconceivable. Yet, was it more incredible than anything else? What other answer could there be? The whole thought was sickening. She pictured him kneeling on the earth, the thin, limp hand in his, pulling and twisting to get the ring off over the knuckle, and a thick, sour liquid rose in her throat and filled the back of her mouth.

"Why?" she asked again.

"I told you the truth, Sue," David said miserably. "I just don't know. I've asked myself that question a hundred times. I just know that when I saw that ring on his hand, there was something about it that made me feel—" He faltered and left the sentence hanging incomplete.

"Feel, how?" Susan pressed him.

"As though—it were—mine," David said haltingly. "It was as though it were something that belonged to me a long time ago, and I had lost it."

"That doesn't make sense," Susan said.

"I know it doesn't. I can't explain it any more than that. I don't understand it any better than you do. I took it, and that's that. Now I've got to get rid of it."

"Why didn't you say something back at the soda shop when Jeff told us about the announcement on the radio?" Susan asked. "Why did you let it stand, when Mark said no one had taken the ring, so the broadcast had to be some sort of trick?"

"I just didn't want to have to hash it over," David said. "Mark was in one of his nasty moods, and I

didn't want to have to explain a lot of stuff I didn'
have answers for. I feel rotten enough for having don
such a dumb thing. I don't need Mark on my bacl
too."

"We can't keep secrets from Mark," Susan said
"Mark has to know everything, or he won't be able t
tell us what to do."

"If Mark knew about the ring," David said, "al
he'd do would be to tell me to get rid of it fast. I'm
going to do that anyway. That's why we're going tc
my house. I'll get it, and on the way over to your place
I'll dump it down a sewer grating or something."

"Where is the ring right now?" Susan asked him.

"In my bedroom," David said, "in the top drawer or
my bureau, in a little box where I keep spare change
and stuff. That's the house, over there, the brown one
on the corner. I'll have the ring in about two minutes."

They covered the distance in silence. When they
reached the house, David said, "The car's not here. I
guess my mother isn't back yet. I'll have to walk you
home."

He turned the knob and shoved the door open, mo-
tioning Susan in ahead of him. She stepped hesitantly
into the small, darkened room, glancing nervously
about her.

"Don't you lock up when nobody's here?"

"My grandmother's always here," David said.

He closed the door hard, and a voice from a back
room immediately called, "Davy? Is that you?"

"Sure, Gram. It's me," David called back. "I've
brought home some company."

"I thought you would!" The shrill, old voice
cracked with a note of excitement. "I told your mother

just a while ago that you'd be doing that. Bring him back here!"

"It's not a him, it's a her," David said. He took Susan's arm and steered her through the living room to the bedroom doorway. "This is Sue McConnell. Sue, this is my gram, Mrs. Ruggles."

"How do you do," Susan said politely to the gray-haired woman in the blue flowered robe.

Mrs. Ruggles stared back at her, blankly.

"Who's she?" she asked David.

"I told you, Gram, she's Sue McConnell. She's a friend from school."

"That's the 'company'?" The woman's pale blue eyes clouded with disappointment.

"That's right," David said. "You two visit a minute while I get something I left in my room. Then I'm walking Sue home."

"I'll come with you," Susan started to say, but David had already left her. There was nothing to do but to move on into the room and stand there awkwardly, trying to smile down at the woman in the chair by the window, though Mrs. Ruggles had now shifted her gaze to the empty doorway.

"There's nobody else?"

"No," Susan said apologetically. "There's just me." Then, as silence grew, she attempted to fill the gap by adding, "We were with a bunch of other people this afternoon, but they didn't come back here with us."

With those words she seemed to reclaim the old woman's attention. The pale eyes focused sharply on Susan's face.

"Did you meet Davy's daddy?"

"No," Susan said, bewildered. "From things David has said, I thought his parents were separated."

"They are, but his daddy's come back," Mrs. Ruggles said. "That's who I thought you were when he said he'd brought 'company.' I knew he wouldn't bring him when *she* was here, but with her gone to the laundry and all, it seemed the right time."

"I don't know anything about that," Susan said. "David hasn't told me anything about his father being in town."

"He is, he is. I've got the proof of it."

There was the sound of footsteps and David appeared abruptly in the doorway. His face was pale and worried.

"Gram," he said, "has anybody been in my room today?"

"Your mother changed the sheets in there. You know it's Saturday."

"Besides that, was anyone in there? I can't find something I had in my bureau."

"Things get lost sometimes," Mrs. Ruggles said. "Especially little things. They can fall down cracks."

"There aren't any cracks in my bureau drawer, and how did you know what size it was?" He regarded her with suspicion. "Gram, have you been into my change box? Tell me the truth now."

"Now, why would I go there?" the old woman asked innocently.

"I don't know. You tell me. Why would you?" He came over and stood beside her chair. "Look, Gram, things don't just disappear into thin air. I had a ring in that box. What happened to it?"

"Perhaps your daddy came and got it?" Mrs. Ruggles suggested.

"My *father?* What do you mean by that?"

"Now, don't you play games with me, Davy Ruggles," his grandmother said. "I know my own boy's college ring when I see it. All the money we spent sending him to that big college in California, I ought to know the ring. I even know the inscription. 'Die Luft der Freiheit Weht,' it says. He used to read it out loud in German and then translate it because he liked it so much. It means 'The winds of freedom blow.' "

"Then it *was* you who got into my things," David accused her.

"I was just going to borrow a couple of dimes to get me a candy bar. You know your mother, she never leaves a single penny anywhere, and a person does get hungry sometimes for a little something sweet."

"I don't care about the money," David said, "I want the ring. What have you done with it?"

"I didn't say I took it."

"Gram, you *did!*" David put his hand on the blue flowered shoulder. "Look, I'll get you a dozen candy bars if you want them, just give the ring back to me. You know you wouldn't like it if I got into your things and took something."

"It wasn't yours, Davy," Mrs. Ruggles said. "It was your daddy's. Your daddy was wearing that ring the day he left here. The only way you could have it is if he's come back again and given it to you. You've been with your daddy. You know where he is. Why are you keeping it a secret?"

"I swear, Gram, that's not my father's ring," David said. "I haven't seen my dad since I was a little kid. You've got things all mixed up."

"I'm an old woman, Davy, and I want to see my boy before I die."

"Then I hope you will, but I can't bring him to you. I didn't get that ring from my father."

"Then where did you get it?" Irma Ruggles asked him.

"I found it."

"Where?"

"On the sidewalk."

"If it's just a found thing, why does it mean so much to you?" The old woman turned to Susan. "Where did Davy get the ring?"

"He found it," Susan said thinly. "Just like he said he did."

"You were with him?"

"Yes. It was lying there on the pavement, and the sun hit it, and the stone sort of caught the light, and David picked it up and said—and said—'Somebody must have dropped this.'" The words came stumbling forth, sounding so contrived to her own ears that she almost strangled on them.

She was not surprised to see the look of disbelief on the wrinkled face.

"There was no stone in the ring," Irma Ruggles said with dignity. "There was a tree inscribed. The German words go all the way around the ring, and the tree is in the middle."

Silence settled heavily upon the room. Susan closed her eyes. When I open them, she told herself, this whole room will have vanished and this dreadful woman with it. Ten years will have gone by, and I will be grown and far away in my private cabin on the shore of a lake. I will look out through my fine window onto deep, calm green, with millions of tiny ripples shining and sparkling in the sunlight, and a breeze will come, clean and sweet across the water, smelling of pine trees. I will think back and ask myself, where was I ten years ago. What was I doing? What was I feeling? And I won't even remember.

But when she opened her eyes once more it was all still there, the cramped room with the two narrow beds stripped of their sheets to reveal the thin, sagging mattresses, the portable television set sitting lifeless on its stand in the corner, the old lady glowering from the depths of her chair. Through the window behind her there was another window and another bedroom and another woman, this one with her hair in curlers. The neighbor woman stared at Susan with undisguised interest and then glanced past her at the unmade beds and began to smile.

"Come on, Sue," David said in a low voice, "I'll walk you home."

"But you haven't gotten what we came for!"

"That's okay. I'll get it later. Gram will change her mind."

No, she won't, Susan thought with a sick sort of despair. She will keep that ring hidden away like a squirrel with a nut, day after day, week after week, while she waits for David to produce his father. And then one day she will realize that the father is not coming, and she will pop forth the ring from under her pillow or out of a cold cream jar or wherever she has put it, and she'll say to David's mother, "Look what Davy says he found on the sidewalk? Though he didn't really find it there, because this girl he brought home with him one day, who was supposed to have been with him when he discovered it, couldn't describe what it looked like. Why did they lie to me about this? Where did he really get it?" And David's mother will say—

She could not force her mind any farther.

"You don't have to walk me," she said to David. "It's not far. I can go home by myself."

"I'd like to take you."

"No—please—I don't want you to." Susan turned quickly away from him. "I'm glad to have met you, Mrs. Ruggles."

Whirling on her heel, Susan rushed through the bedroom doorway and stumbled through the living room, bruising her shins against the edge of a coffee table that was lost in a shadow pocket by a plastic-covered sofa. She pushed past a chair and a telephone stand, and found the door to the outside. She pulled it open and burst through, and the soft, spring dusk came upon her in a gush of cool air and golden, slanted light.

The car that David had driven the times he picked her up at the house was parked at the curb, and a tall woman with thick, dark hair was lifting a laundry basket from the backseat. Another time Susan would have looked at her curiously, but now she sped by with hardly a glance, intent only on putting distance between herself and the place she was leaving.

Halfway down the block she began to run, grateful for the cold purity of the wind against the heat of her face.

That is where David lives, she thought incredulously. That is where he goes when he leaves school in the afternoon. That place and the people in it are his life!

"The winds of freedom blow," Susan thought, and she could have wept for him, but the panic that had started to build within her now began to take her over.

David's grandmother was not dumb. She was old, yes, and confused, but there had been a sharpness in her eyes and a craftiness in the way she had managed to twist the conversation that denied stupidity. David would not have an easy time getting the ring away from her. That much Susan knew with certainty. With the ring in her possession, and among the shifting lights and shadows of her faded mind, Mrs. Irma Ruggles was dangerous.

We've got to do something, but what? Susan asked herself frantically. David could not handle the situation alone, and she herself could do nothing to help him.

There was one person who would know what to do, one person who always knew what to do.

Susan entered her house by the front door and went straight through the hall to the stairs. She could hear the voices of her father and brothers, raised in friendly argument in the den; from the kitchen there came the clink of pans and dishes. The warm, familiar odors of the dinner hour filled the stairwell.

Susan went up the stairs and down the hall to the phone. She looked up a number in the directory, lifted the receiver, and dialed.

A woman's voice answered.

"Hello, is this Mrs. Garrett?" Susan said. "I'm trying to get in touch with Mark Kinney. Is he there with Jeff? Oh, good. Please, can I speak to him?"

SIXTEEN

The Sunday paper carried the complete story.

"Terrible," Mr. McConnell said. "Utterly unbelievable. What kind of maniac would do such a thing! What sort of motive could there have been? The man wasn't carrying anything of value. All that was missing when they found him were a couple of dollars and his Stanford class ring."

"His poor wife!" Mrs. McConnell exclaimed. "With a baby coming! How dreadful this is for her! It says the funeral will be on Tuesday. You will be going to it, won't you, Sue?"

"No," Susan said. "Mother, I just can't."

She could not shift her gaze from the photograph on the front page. The picture was not a recent one, for it lacked a mustache, and devoid of this protective camouflage the mouth looked young and oddly vulnerable. What could not be denied were the eyes. Susan had looked into those cool, challenging eyes five mornings a week for the past school year.

Good morning, class.

Good morning, Mr. Griffin.

"Sue, dear," her mother said, "I know how you feel and how hard it must be for you, but I really feel you ought to go. It's bound to mean something to his wife to see that his students were fond enough of him to turn out for his funeral. Perhaps Dad and I should go with you. After all, Mrs. Griffin was here in our home just the other night."

"Does it say how he was killed?" Craig asked with interest.

"They're doing an autopsy. There were bruises on the body, but no other signs of violence." Mr. McConnell was scanning the story. "He had a history of heart-related problems, so they think it's possible he suffered coronary arrest.

"This says police were led to the discovery of the body in 'a secluded area of the Sandias' by a girl named Lana Turnboldt. She and a former boyfriend used to go hiking in the area. Yesterday she was up there with her fiancé for a picnic and found a medicine vial with Griffin's name on it and a few yards away a patch of newly turned earth. She reported this to the police who investigated and found it was a grave."

"Do you feel real bad, Sue?" Melvynne asked respectfully. "I never knew anybody who got dead."

"Of course, she feels bad," his mother said, putting her arm around Susan's shoulders. "It's a tragic thing. I just pray whoever did this will be caught and punished to the full limit of the law."

"The one clue they mention is a blue Windbreaker that was wrapped around the body," Mr. McConnell said. "It was a man's size, small. It says, 'Detective James Baca who is in charge of the investigation said there were no identifying marks on the jacket. "It came from Sears. Millions of people wear these things," Baca said.' "

"We ought to send flowers," Mrs. McConnell said. "The shops will be closed today, but I'll order some in the morning." She gave her daughter a squeeze and released her and went over to the stove. "How many want eggs this morning?"

"John, I want to talk with you about something," Paula Garrett said. "Jeff has been up since dawn working out in the garage on Mark Kinney's car."

"So?" her husband grunted.

"Tear yourself away from the income tax and listen to me a moment. This is Sunday, Jeff's one day to relax. He has practice tomorrow and Tuesday, and Wednesday night is the last day of the tournament."

"So?" John Garrett said again. "Jeff never misses practice."

"I know. That's just my point. He throws himself so hard into his sports activities, he needs to get rest when he can. Mark takes advantage of their friendship to a point where it's disgraceful, and as far as I can see, Jeff never gets anything back from it. It's all give on one side and all take on the other."

"You worry too much," John Garrett said. "What's this about Mark Kinney's car, anyway? I didn't think the kid had a car. If he's got his own wheels, how come Jeff drives him around all the time?"

"Mark just bought the car, or I guess he did," Paula said. "It's a beat-up old thing, purely secondhand. He and Betsy came over in it yesterday afternoon and drove it straight into the garage. Jeff says he's going to help him fix it up, but there's no 'helping' about it. Mark got a phone call from some girl a couple of minutes after he got here and took off immediately. Now this morning Jeff's out there painting that car all by himself, and it's not even his."

"Jeff likes working on cars. He had some other kid's car out there for a while last month. You didn't hit the roof over that."

"No, I didn't, because Greg Dart was out there with him working right alongside him, and besides that, he paid Jeff for his work. You can be sure Mark isn't going to fork over a penny. I bet Jeff's even buying the paint."

"They've been friends for a long time, Paula."

"I know," Jeff's mother said. "I can remember the first time he brought Mark home with him. I thought then that their friendship couldn't last a week. That weird little weasel of a boy and our Jeff—why, they had nothing in common. Jeff would be out back shooting baskets, and Mark would be slouching against a tree, staring off into space like he was half asleep. I thought Jeff was just being kind because the boy was new in town and didn't have parents."

"Well, likely he was," her husband said. "And I think it shows the goodness in Jeff that he's continued to help the kid. From the things Mark's let drop when he's been over here, I gather he's got no kind of home life. He's got an uncle who beats him and an aunt who won't fix his meals; the only nourishment he gets comes from that greasy-spoon soda shop or out of our refrigerator. No wonder he's attached himself to a solid, well-adjusted guy like Jeff. It's his anchor in life."

"Maybe so," Paula said more slowly. "I could be over-reacting. It's just that I've never been able to get really fond of Mark. He and Jeff are together so much, and he's in and out of here every day, and he's

polite enough, but I don't feel I know him at all as a
person. Do you?"

"I never thought about it," John Garrett said.
"Maybe there's not much there to know. The kid's a
shadow of Jeff, trailing along in his footsteps. It's kind
of pitiful actually, since he'll never be able to begin to
measure up to him. You can tell he's got a crush on
Betsy, but what girl would look twice at him with Jeff
around? It's sort of sad."

"Well, when you put it that way," Paula said. "I
guess Jeff's a big enough boy now to handle his own
relationships. It's up to the strong in this life to take
care of the weak, isn't it? And our boy's pretty special."

"Darned right he is," John Garrett said, turning
back to his tax return. "All you have to do is open the
paper or pick up a magazine, and you see a bunch of
messed-up kids in trouble. It makes you wonder where
the parents are while all that's going on."

Kathy Griffin lay on her back, staring at the ceiling. She had slept, dreamless, through the night as a
result of the sedative they had given her. When she
wakened, it had been slowly, in stages. Consciousness
had inched upon her, first with the knowledge that
she was no longer sleeping, then as she automatically
turned and reached into the bed beside her.

It was empty.

He's up ahead of me, she had thought drowsily, but
even as the words formed in her mind she had known
there was something wrong with them. There were no
sounds of movement in the room, no thumps of bureau drawers being opened and closed. The shower
was not running in the bathroom. There was no hum
of an electric razor.

Where is Brian? And then, quickly, she had shoved the question away. I will not ask myself now. I'm not ready to think about that yet. Desperately she tried to shove herself back into the safe cocoon of oblivion, but it had sealed itself behind her. I must sleep—I have to sleep some more! But while her arms and legs lay weighted upon the mattress, and her body remained a leaden lump, too heavy to think of lifting, her mind kept opening, inch by dreadful inch.

Where is Brian? Where—is—Brian? Where——is—— he?

I—know. I——know.

There was a crack in the ceiling over the bed. Brian had been planning to fix it during Easter vacation. "It won't take much. Just some sort of plaster filler."

"You'll never get around to that and you know it. You have a million books you're going to read that week."

"Well, I'll make the sacrifice. I'll hold myself down to a million minus one, and fix the ceiling. We can't have the whole roof caving in on top of Brian Junior."

In the far corner of the room there was a cobweb, a wisp of lace caught in a beam of morning sunlight. Had some industrious spider created that masterpiece overnight, or had it been there, unnoticed, for days? It was strange the things you saw when you looked at the ceiling—really concentrated on it to the exclusion of everything else. The plaster ran in waves and swirls, and here and there, there were little lumps in it, as though it had been spread too slowly and had dried before it was smoothed. "People who do halfway jobs shouldn't do them at all," Brian said. If Brian had been a plasterer, the swirls in the ceiling would have been symmetrical and all the lumps would have been smoothed away.

Where——is——Brian——I——know——I——know.

I——know.

Somewhere in the house a telephone rang. It rang only once.

A moment later the bedroom door opened a crack and then came open wider.

"Oh—you're awake," a woman's voice said.

"Semiawake," Kathy said. "I feel like I've got a hangover."

"There's a telegram from your parents. They're getting an afternoon flight and will be in late this evening." The owner of the voice came into the room and stood next to the bed. "What can I get you, hon? Coffee?"

"I don't know. Yes, coffee, I guess. You haven't been here all night, have you, Rose?"

"Of course I have. What are neighbors for if not to be on hand when—things happen?" The woman said, "There have been a lot of phone calls already. Brian's principal called, and several of the teachers, and some professor at the college who said he was head of the English Department there. I've kept a list of the names."

"That's good of you, Rose." Kathy pulled herself, with effort, to a sitting position. "Well, Brian Junior's still with us. He just kicked me a good one. How do they all know about it? Is it in the paper?"

"There's a big write-up on the front page," Rose said. "They even have Brian's picture, though it doesn't look much like him without the mustache. I don't know where they got that."

"It was probably taken back when he was at the university. They must have got it out of a yearbook file or something." Her tongue felt thick and her head ached to fall back onto the pillow. "Can I see it?"

"You don't want to read it all, hon. It'll only upset you."

"What is, is," Kathy said. "Reading about it isn't going to make it any worse. Maybe when I read it, it will go into some sort of perspective. Maybe it will start to make sense. Who could possibly hate Brian enough to do this thing? What kind of person hates like that?"

"They'll find him. That's what police are for."

"But they don't know where to start. All they could talk about was the Windbreaker. There has to be something more than that, some better starting place. When I was with them yesterday I must have been in shock. I couldn't think. Everything they said to me seemed to run in and out of my brain like water. I kept trying to grab hold of things, but they kept sliding away from me before I could put them together to make any sort of meaning."

"That was a blessing, maybe."

"There was something—the name of somebody—that meant something to me. I remember having a feeling of recognition when I heard it. I started to tell them, and then I couldn't remember any longer what it was I was going to say."

The telephone rang again, clearer, now that the bedroom door was open.

"I'll get that," Rose said, "and then I'll bring you coffee."

"And the paper," Kathy said.

At eleven-ten on Sunday morning, Mrs. Irma Ruggles sat in a chair by her bedroom window and played with the circle of gold on the fourth finger of her right hand. First she turned it so she could see the tree and read the German words; then she released it and let its own weight twist the ring so that all she could see was the band.

The ring was loose on her finger, but not too terribly loose. If it had been even a fraction of an inch smaller it might have been difficult sliding it over her knuckle.

Whoever this is has a thin hand for a man, thought Mrs. Ruggles, turning the ring again so that the tree appeared on top.

She could not have said exactly when it was that she had stopped thinking of the ring as belonging to her son and had inserted a nameless owner in his place. Yesterday morning, when she had found it in David's bureau, she had been so certain that he had gotten it from his father. The shock of seeing it there, among the dimes and nickels and tie tacks and shirt studs in the box she always visited for candy money, had jolted her terribly. It had been like hearing her son's voice crying out to her across the years.

But later, when she had confronted David with her suspicions, things had not occurred as she had expected. He had been rattled, yes, and he had certainly acted guilty, but not guilty as a boy might be who had a glorious secret. "I haven't seen my dad since I was a little kid," he had told her, and the words had rung true. David was not good at deception. He could not have falsified the pain in his voice, any more than he could have injected convincing sincerity into his next statement: "I found it."

And the girl—the plain, mousy, bespectacled girl, who was so exactly the opposite of any girl she would ever have picked for David—that girl had lied so badly that anyone with half a brain could have realized she was not telling the truth. And then, the look on her face when she had been told, "There was no stone in the ring. There was a tree"! Her eyes had gotten a wild, glazed look, and then she had closed them and stood there, silent, as though wishing herself a million miles away.

Irma had not accepted it then, perhaps because she did not want to accept it. But little by little in the long hours since, the dream had fallen away. Her son was not in town. He would not turn up suddenly on the doorstep, his beautiful face alight with joy and love. Her David, the first David, had vanished from their lives with the finality of a bright bird flying straight into the sun, leaving nothing behind him but the memory of a feathered touch and the rustle of restless wings. She would not see him again in this world and perhaps, if the things the Reverend Chandler preached were true, not anywhere.

"Those who refuse to shoulder their earthly burdens will never know the glory of everlasting life," the reverend had said straight from the pulpit seven years ago, and Irma had refused to attend church since.

This had upset her daughter-in-law terribly.

"He didn't mean anything personal, Mother Ruggles," she had said. "My goodness, with the hundreds of people he has in his congregation, he can't stop and worry about the effect every single thing he says will have on every one of them. How's it going to look, if you stop attending services with David and me? Why, people will think I won't take the trouble to bring you."

"They won't think that," Irma had told her. "They know how responsible you are. Just tell them I'm feeling poorly."

"Every Sunday?"

"I'm an old woman. When you get old, you can feel poorly whenever you want to." She had meant this as a little joke, but her daughter-in-law had not found it amusing. The fact was, she seldom found anything amusing. Irma was sure that was one main reason why Big David had left her. The winds of freedom are filled with laughter.

But now she was wandering. She knew she did that lately; concentration became more difficult when you grew old. The thing she wanted to think about now was the ring. If David had not found it and had not gotten it from his father, then where had it come from? He was not going to tell her, that was evident, and his refusal was a challenge to her innate stubbornness.

This morning he had come to her again, scrubbed and shining, dressed in his church clothes, as handsome as his father had ever been as a boy, and had said, "Gram, please let me have it."

"Have what?" she had asked with feigned puzzlement, knowing that his mother was right in the next room and wondering if he would mention it in her hearing.

He wouldn't.

"You know," he had said in a low voice. "Gram, look, it's really important to me. You don't know how important. It belongs to somebody, and I have to give it back to him."

"To who?"

"You don't know him, Gram. His name wouldn't mean anything to you. Where are you keeping it? If you'll get it for me, I'll—"

"David, aren't you ready yet?" his mother had called from the living room. "We're going to be late and have to sit in the back."

And so he had gone, glancing back at her with a pleading, worried look as he left, and she had experienced a subtle shift in her own emotions. David was honestly upset, as upset as she had ever seen him. And the girl had been also. There was something very wrong here, somehow.

Where had this ring come from, and why was it so important?

She was back to the beginning again. She turned the ring slowly on her finger, staring at it as though the answer might suddenly appear interspersed with the words of German. Could David have stolen the ring? Such a thing was hard to imagine, but young people today did seem to be under all kinds of intense pressures that drove them to do strange and unpredictable things. Davy didn't have much spending money, and now that he was beginning to date, this might be suddenly important. At the same time, common sense told you that if you were going to steal for money, there were all sorts of things more marketable than a college ring.

Lost in contemplation, Irma Ruggles did not hear the front door open, only the sharp click as it was shoved closed. Could time have passed so quickly? She glanced up, startled.

"Davy," she called, "is that you?"

There was no answer.

"Davy?" she said again, turning to face the figure that had appeared silently in the bedroom doorway, and then she stopped, bewildered. Her hands rose with a jerk which sent the ring sliding off her finger, into her lap.

"Why, you're not Davy!" she said to the boy with the funny eyes.

SEVENTEEN

The wind began in the early afternoon. It rose slowly at first, but increased steadily, as winds do in the Southwest in March, lifting the dust from the vacant lots and unpaved roads and mesas and sending it sweeping into the town.

The Sunday twilight was muted and pink, as the sun's last rays slanted through the thick, red air, and when dark came the wind did not drop but seemed to grow stronger, whining around the corners of houses and stripping the first new leaf buds from the trees.

Susan brought two logs in from the pile beside the garage and built a fire. She felt foolish doing it, for the evening was not cold, but some inner part of her seemed to be freezing. It took some time before she could get the fire to catch; this chore had always fallen to Craig or her father. Once she got it going she sat on the floor, huddled as close as she could get to the fire screen, taking comfort as much from the friendly, crackling sound as from the heat of the flames.

"Are you sure you won't change your mind and come with us?" her mother had asked one final time before they had left. "I know how low you're feeling, but Sunday suppers at the church are always fun, and seeing other people might give you a lift."

"I'm sure," Susan had told her. "I just couldn't face it."

"There's going to be a sing-along," Francis had reminded her.

"I said, I don't want to come."

The thought of the crowded church basement with her parents' friends chattering and munching and hordes of shrieking children racing about between the long, food-covered tables had in itself been enough to exhaust her. Now, alone in the house, she wondered if she had made a mistake in not going. Although she dreamed often of solitude, she had seldom actually experienced it. With the comings and goings of a large family, the McConnell house was seldom empty and almost never silent. Tonight its absolute stillness, accentuated by the moan of the wind outside, was oppressive and almost frightening.

Hungry suddenly for the sound of human voices, Susan turned on the television and flicked the dial from channel to channel. On one a comedian and his newly divorced wife were trading insults; on another a female singer was wailing about the agony of lost love.

Ironically, on the third channel, the first words she heard were "Brian Griffin."

". . . for Brian Griffin, Del Norte English teacher, whose body was found yesterday in a shallow grave in the Sandia Mountains. Results of the autopsy show the cause of death to have been coronary arrest, possibly preceded by a severe angina attack. Griffin's wrists and ankles were bound with twine, tightly enough to obstruct circulation to the hands and feet, and there were bruises on his arms and legs, the coroner's report said.

"Mrs. Katherine Griffin, the wife of the deceased, said that a new prescription for the medication Griffin took for angina was on order at the . . ."

Susan turned off the set.

In the kitchen, in a pan on the back of the stove, was stew from last night's dinner. Her mother had set it out for her before she had left.

"Be sure to eat, Sue," she had told her, and Susan had nodded agreement.

Now she went out to the kitchen and stood for a moment in front of the stove, trying to decide if she would be able to face a meal. The mere smell of the food, with its combination of onion and spices, made her slightly nauseated. She had almost decided to put the whole concoction down the disposal, when the doorbell rang.

"Who in the world—" Susan hesitated, feeling reluctant to open the door when she was alone in the house. Then she thought of David. Of course, it would be he, come to give her a follow-up on the situation with the ring. By this time Mark would have talked with him, and perhaps they would have worked out a solution.

Setting the stew pan back on the burner, Susan went to the door and opened it. To her surprise, she found her visitors to be Jeff and Betsy.

"Are you here alone?" Betsy asked, glancing quickly about her.

"Yes," Susan said. "The rest of the family is out for the evening."

"Well, good. We can talk then. Aren't you going to ask us in?"

"Of course. Come in," Susan said, stepping back to

allow them to enter. Both their faces were red from the wind, and Betsy's hair was wild around her face.

"We're on our way to Zuni," Jeff said. "I got the car sprayed gray this morning, and Betsy's borrowed the license off her mom's VW to use on the drive out there. We figure nobody will be using the bug tonight, and we'll get the license back on again before anybody sees it in the morning."

"How are you going to get back?" Susan asked them.

"We've got Griffin's car," Betsy said. "And Mark's going to follow us in Jeff's. After we dump the Chevy we'll come back with him. He's going to meet us here in a couple of minutes. The reason we stopped here is to tell you that I told my folks I was spending the night with you. I don't think Mom will check it out, but if she does happen to call about something, you'll have to handle it."

"How?" Susan asked nervously.

"Oh, for Christ's sake—you're supposed to be so smart; figure out something. Tell her I'm asleep or in the bathtub or whatever. The main thing is to be sure you get the phone every time it rings tonight. That won't be hard considering your folks are out."

"The other thing is, we've got to get hold of Dave," Jeff said. "I gave my folks the same story about sleeping at his house. Are you going to see him tonight?"

"Not that I know of," Susan said.

"We tried to stop at his place on the way over here," Betsy told her, "but there was a whole line of cars parked in front like they were giving a party. We didn't think we ought to go in."

"Let's call him from here," Jeff said. "Do you know his number, Sue?"

"No," Susan said, "but I can look it up. There's a

phone in the den." She led the way into the wood-paneled room where the fire was burning brightly and casting dancing shadows against the far wall.

"I'll find it," Jeff said, picking up the phone directory, which lay on a stand under the wall phone. "I'll read the numbers out to you, and you dial. It'll sound more natural if the call comes from you. Are you ready? Two-six-eight—"

Susan shoved the numbers into place. There was a connecting click, and the phone on the other end of the line began to ring. After a moment a woman's voice answered.

"Hello," Susan said. "Could I speak to David, please?"

"Can I tell him who's calling?" the woman asked.

"It's Susan."

"Okay. Just a minute." The voice moved away from the phone. "It's somebody named Susan for David. Does he want to take a call right now?" From somewhere in the background there was an answer. Susan was aware of the hum of numerous voices. There was a long pause, and then the sound of the receiver being lifted and David's voice.

"Hello?"

"David, it's Sue." She was not sure he understood it was she who was calling. "What's happening over there? Is something the matter?"

"Yes," David said in a flat voice. "My grandmother died this morning."

"Oh, David!" She was stunned. "How awful!"

"Yeah, it is pretty awful. It happened while my mother and I were at church. We found her lying on the floor in the bedroom. She must have fallen and hit her head when she was getting out of her chair."

"How awful," Susan said again. "Is there anything I can do?" The question was ridiculous, and she knew it, but it was the only thing she could think of to say.

"No," David said. "What is it you called about?" He was far away from her, so far away there was no way to touch him. Susan found herself wondering if she would ever touch him again. The scene yesterday in the bedroom between themselves and the old, gray-haired woman would stand between them forever. It would be a memory David would want to thrust away from him, and in her presence, it would come surging back to be relived, over and over again.

She answered his question.

"Jeff and Betsy are here. They're on their way to take the Chevy out to the pueblo. Jeff has told his parents he's spending the night with you and wants you to cover him if they should try to call him there."

"I can't do that," David said. "Our minister's over here and half the people from the church. It's a regular wake. None of them have seen Gram for years, but you'd never know it to listen to them. There's no way I can catch the phone when it rings. One of my mom's friends is acting as telephone secretary."

"Oh," Susan said. "Well, Jeff will just have to change his story. David, the ring—" It was not the right time to ask it, but she could not let him forget. "Have you gotten it yet?"

"I don't want to think about that right now," David said.

"But, David, you have to! What if somebody else finds it? It has to be there somewhere in the bedroom."

"I'll hunt through her stuff, but not tonight. There's too much going on over here." He dropped his voice. "The spacy woman from next door came over a few minutes ago, and you know what she said? That there was a guy in the bedroom with Gram at the time she died. She said she looked across from her bedroom window and saw him standing talking to Gram back behind her chair. She didn't think anything about it at the time, because she thought it was me."

"But—but—how could there have been anybody?" Susan stammered.

"There couldn't have been, of course, but she's got my mom and everybody else here all riled up. She says the guy was wearing a brown sweater. I don't even own a brown sweater."

"How much did she see?" Susan asked shakily. "Did she actually see your grandmother fall?"

"No. She says she looked over once and saw this guy with Gram and then later she looked again and Gram wasn't in her chair anymore and she didn't see anybody. She's got to be making the whole thing up. Gram didn't have drop-in visitors, and if she did have they sure wouldn't have been teenage guys. I think the woman's cracked. She's using this as a way to get some attention for herself."

"But what if it was a burglar?" Susan said. "Is anything missing from the house?"

"Nope. My mom's jewelry, such as it is, is all in its box, and there's nothing else here that anybody would want to steal. Look, I've got to get back to my mother now. She's taking this pretty hard." David's voice came from years away. "Did you want anything else?"

"No," Susan said. "I just called about the alibi for Jeff. David—" She sought for words and could not find them. "I'm sorry," she said lamely.

"Yeah—well, so am I. She was quite an old girl, my gram. The place is going to seem pretty strange."

"Yes, I imagine so."

"Good-bye," David said.

"Good-bye."

Susan replaced the receiver on the hook. Jeff and Betsy were looking at her questioningly.

"His grandmother died today," Susan said.

"Well, what about the cover?" Jeff asked.

"He said he can't do it."

"Shit, that really messes us up if my folks try to get hold of me. Well, there's nothing to do but take the chance, I guess." He paused, taking in the expression on Susan's face. "Hey, what's with you? You look like you're going to keel over."

"Mark has a brown sweater," Susan said. "He wears it all the time."

"What's that supposed to mean?"

"It means—it means—" Susan felt the floor tilting strangely beneath her. The room swam about her, and she reached out a hand to brace herself against the wall for support. "When I told Mark about the ring—he said—'Don't worry. I'll get it.' And there was someone with her when she died. The woman in the house next door saw him."

"You're not making sense," Betsy said. "What ring was Mark going to get?"

"Mr. Griffin's ring, the one that was missing from his finger when they found him. David took it."

"Dave did?" Jeff said in surprise. "My gosh, why?"

"Because—because—" She could not try to explain. That part no longer mattered. All that was important now was the horrendous realization that was sweeping over her. "Mark killed that woman. He went over there this morning while David and his mother were in church, and he took the ring from her, and he killed her!"

"You're crazy," Betsy said. "Mark would never do a thing like that."

"He would, and he did!" Suddenly, incredibly, there was no doubt in her mind. "We've got to go to the police!"

"Bets is right, you *are* crazy," Jeff said. "After all we've gone through to keep this under cover, you think we're going to go to the pigs *now*? Why, we'd have to tell them everything right from the beginning, the whole bit about the kidnapping and Griffin's dying on us and the burial, and who would ever believe it was an accident, especially if you're going to follow it up with this wild thing about Dave's grandmother?"

"It's gone past the point where there's any choice," Susan said. "Whatever they do to us, they'll just have to do."

"You don't have the right to make that decision," Betsy said. "We're all of us in this together. You agreed to help in the kidnapping, and by doing that, you agreed to anything that followed from it. You're committed, just like the rest of us. You can't chicken out now."

"Didn't you hear a thing I said?" Susan asked her. "Mark killed Mrs. Ruggles! *He killed an old woman!* Mr. Griffin's death was an accident, but this wasn't. Mark knew what he was doing. He planned it, and he killed her."

"You don't know that," Jeff said. "You don't have proof."

"I do know it, and I don't need proof! The police can find that!" Susan was on the edge of hysteria. "If I'm wrong, if Mark had nothing to do with this, if it really was an accident and the old lady slipped and fell, that will show up from her injuries. They can do an autopsy on her the same way they did on Mr. Griffin. But if he did do it—"

"If he did do it, he did it to protect us, you as well as the rest of us," Betsy said. "He was willing to take that risk in order to keep us safe. If Dave was stupid enough to take that ring and let his grandmother get hold of it, what could Mark do but get it back any way he could?"

"But to *murder* someone—"

"Like Jeff said, you're only guessing about that, and you're probably wrong. But if you're not, just remember that Mark did only what he had to do. He's gotten us through this far, and we've got to trust him to get us through the rest of the way."

"I don't care what you say," Susan said miserably, "I'm going to the police, and I'm going to tell them everything. After that, whatever happens, happens. I'm sorry if the two of you won't back me up, but if you think Mark did only what he had to do, then you can believe the same thing about me. I can't go on like this any longer. It's like a snowball rolling downhill; it's getting worse all the time!"

From the street outside there came the quick, impatient beep of a car horn.

"That's Mark," Betsy said. "What are we going to do?"

"It won't do us any good to get rid of the car if Miss Holier-Than-Thou is going to spill the beans," Jeff said. "We've got to keep her quiet."

"How?"

"I'll stay here with her. You run out and tell Mark what's happened. He'll think of something."

"You can't tell Mark!" Susan cried. "He's the very one—"

But Jeff's hand was clamped tightly upon her shoulder, and Betsy was already out the door.

When she returned a few moments later, Mark was with her. He was still wearing the brown sweater.

EIGHTEEN

Where's her family?" Mark asked.

"Out for the evening," Jeff said. "There's nobody else here."

"Good. Let's tie her up. The cord on those drapes will do fine. Betsy, go out to the kitchen and get something to cut them with."

"Betsy, no!" Susan twisted in Jeff's grip so that she faced the other girl squarely. "You can't keep doing everything he says, not when you know what he's done!"

"I don't know that he's done anything," Betsy said.

"You don't *want* to know!"

"I said, go get a knife." Mark shifted his gaze from Betsy to Susan. "Now, exactly what is it you're trying to sell them? What am I supposed to have done?"

"You killed David's grandmother," Susan said.

"Did Dave tell you that?"

"No, of course not. He doesn't even realize you knew about his grandmother having the ring. *I* told you that." The implications of this last statement struck her with full force. "*I did that.*"

"And that's all you're going on, that I knew she had the ring? You knew it too, baby." He regarded her quizzically. "If your reasoning holds, that could mean that *you* killed her."

"The woman next door saw you. That is, she saw somebody—a boy in a brown sweater—in the room with Mrs. Ruggles right before it happened."

"How could she see that?"

"Through the window. The house next door has a window exactly opposite the one in Mrs. Ruggles's room," Susan caught her breath in a half sob. "It was you. It couldn't have been anyone else."

"So maybe it was me. I went over and got the ring, like I told you I would. Why does that have to mean I killed the old bag?" He glanced back at Betsy. "You don't think I did that, do you, Bets?"

"No," Betsy said softly. "No."

"Good." Mark nodded approvingly. "Old people fall down, you know? It happens all the time. An old lady tries to jump up out of her chair and stumbles, and down she goes, smacking her head on the windowsill. I ask you, what could I do about it? I wasn't near enough to catch her."

"Nothing," Betsy said. "You couldn't do anything. Not if it happened like that." She turned and went out to the kitchen. There was the sound of drawers being pulled out and the rattle of silverware.

Betsy came back into the room carrying a paring knife.

"Will this do okay?"

"It's not the sharpest thing I've ever seen, but it'll do for a curtain cord." Mark took the knife from her hand and went over to the window.

Held immobile by the grip of Jeff's hands, Susan stood, watching as Mark sawed at the cord of the heavy white drapes that were her mother's pride and joy. "They're the most impractical things I've ever seen," Mr. McConnell had said when she bought them. "They'll have to be cleaned every other month," and Mrs. McConnell had said, "Oh, I don't think it will be quite that bad," but it had been.

What are they going to do to me? Susan thought, terrified, and at the same time there was some odd, untouched corner of her mind that was saying, Mother will be so upset about the draperies, surely there's something else he can use besides those.

"What do we do now?" Jeff asked as Mark came over to them with the cord in his hand.

"Tie her, the way we did Griffin. Put her wrists behind her."

"And then what?" Jeff loosed his hold on Susan's shoulder and as she twisted to jerk away from him he pulled her arms back roughly. An idea occurred to him. "Hey, you're not thinking of doing the same thing with her are you? Leaving her in the mountains? I don't want to be part of that."

"You're part of whatever we do, boy," Mark said easily. He looped the cord around Susan's wrists and pulled it so tight that she gasped in pain. "But, no, that's not the plan. It's too close to the other. People would put two and two together too fast."

"Then what?"

"Lay her down," Mark said, "and help me get her ankles. Hey, you, watch it!" as Susan's foot shot out at him. "You kick me and you're going to be one sorry chick, I'll tell you!"

"Down you go," Jeff said, lifting her easily and laying her squirming body flat on the den floor. He dropped to his knees and bent to pull her legs tightly together. "You want to try to gag her?"

"No sweat. With the noise that wind's making, she could yell her head off and neighbors wouldn't hear her." Mark knotted the cord around Susan's ankles and then drew it up to the wrist cord so that her legs were bent sharply at the knees. "That'll keep her from rolling around and getting into trouble. Okay, you two"—he nodded at Jeff and Betsy—"off to Zuni!"

"To Zuni?" Betsy exclaimed in bewilderment. "Now?"

"What do you mean, 'now'? We're half an hour behind schedule. That isn't going to hurt anything though. We're keeping to the plan. Take the car out there, and I'll pick you up in Jeff's."

"But what about Sue?" Betsy asked. "We're just going to leave her here? What about when her parents come home? As soon as they're in the door she'll tell them everything that happened."

"I don't think she'll do that."

"Why not?" Jeff asked. "What's going to stop her? Look here, Mark, I'm not going to be the one in that Chevy when the sirens start wailing."

"They won't be wailing," Mark said irritably. "I told you, she's not going to set the cops on us. I guarantee it. What's the matter, good buddy, don't you trust me?"

"Sure," Jeff said, "except I want to know what's happening. I'm not going to get off there on the interstate with that car under me without having any idea what the score is."

"Then take your own car, dammit," Mark said. "I'll drive the Chevy. Just get a move on, will you? We want to get back before morning."

"Trust him, Jeff," Betsy said. "Mark knows what he's doing."

"Jeff, please!" Susan said imploringly. "Don't leave me here alone with him!"

"I want to know how you're going to make sure Sue doesn't talk," Jeff said stubbornly. "Like I said, I don't want to get out on that highway—"

"You won't be risking a thing," Mark told him. His voice was tightly controlled, but his eyes were beginning to take on a glint like cold steel. The lids had slipped down so that only the pupils showed, small black dots in the half-moons of gray iris. "I told you, I'll drive the Chevy. If anybody is taking a risk, I'm the one. You and Betsy will be in your car, just as legal as legal. If you get stopped you show the registration, and you're fine."

"How could we explain what we were doing out there a couple of hundred miles from home?" Jeff asked.

"Nobody's going to ask you that." Mark's anger was beginning to surface. "If anybody did, you could say you were eloping. That would shake your folks up enough so they'd never think to ask you anything else." He got to his feet. "I'm telling you for the last time, boy, I'll handle things. I've done all right up till now, haven't I? After you leave, Sue and I are going to have a little talk, and when we're through she will have changed her mind about everything. Sue's not a disloyal person, not basically. She's just gotten a little mixed up on her values."

"You think you can convince her?" Jeff asked doubtfully.

"Sure, he can," Betsy said. "He convinced her the last time, didn't he, after she and Dave found Mr. Griffin? If he could do it then, he can do it now."

"Okay." Jeff fumbled in his pocket and drew out a key. "This is for the Chevy."

"Jeff, please—" Susan tried again in desperation.

"I left your keys in the car. I didn't think we'd be tied up here so long." Mark took the key from Jeff's hand. "Stop worrying. Leave things to me. Okay?"

"Okay," Jeff said again. "Well, I'll go on then. You ready, Bets?"

"I've been ready for ages," Betsy said. She flashed Susan a sudden, bright smile that seemed to come full-blown out of nowhere. "You listen to Mark, Sue. Remember, he knows best."

"I—hate—you," Susan whispered. She did not mean it to be a whisper, but in her twisted position she found she could get no breath to accelerate her voice. "I—hate—you—all."

"We're not too fond of you either, little snot," Betsy said, her smile fading. "Come on, Jeff, let Mark take care of her."

They left. Susan heard the front door open and close.

Then there was silence.

It was not the same silence that had filled the house earlier in the evening, for this time she was not alone. Mark had moved to the other side of her, and Susan had to lift and turn her head in order to see him.

"You're not going to talk me into anything," she said.

"I'm not going to waste my time trying," Mark said.

"What are you going to do?"

"I'm going to open the windows and let in a little air," he told her.

It was not an easy thing to open the draperies with the cord gone, but he managed it by sliding them along the rods by hand. Then he unlatched the windows and raised them as high as they would go. The wind came sweeping into the room with all its stinging, dust-laden force, knocking the shade askew on a lamp at the end of the sofa and sending a figurine on the mantel crashing onto the floor.

The flames leapt high in the fireplace, sending a spray of sparks out through the screen.

"Watch out," Susan gasped. "You'll set the house on fire."

"Setting fire to a place isn't that easy," Mark said lightly. "It takes more work than that."

"What do you mean?"

"You've got to get the curtains started. That's what makes a place really go up. That's what happened to our house back when I was living in Denver; first the curtains and then—whoosh!—the whole thing!"

"I know," Susan said. "You told me. That's how your father died, and I'm sorry. Mark, please, cut me loose! These cords hurt terribly! They're cutting right through the skin!"

"Don't be sorry," Mark said, ignoring the rest of her statement. "He had it coming. You know what that bastard was going to do? Have me stuck in the J.D. home."

"Why?" Susan mouthed the question without interest. Was this how Mr. Griffin had felt lying there by the stream, hour after endless hour? Oh, please, I hope it wasn't, she thought wretchedly. I hope he fainted or went unconscious or something so he couldn't feel any longer.

"Because this guy and I wrote some checks and signed his name," Mark said. "They weren't even for all that much, and the old man could afford to cover them, but do you think he would? No way, not my good old dad. To the wolves with the kid, he said, even if the kid was his only son."

"Mark, please untie me!"

"So you can run to the pigs? You must think I'm pretty stupid. Why would I let you do that?"

"Because you have to," Susan said with more bravado than she felt. "My parents will be home in an hour or so, and I'll tell then anyway. Keeping me tied like this for that length of time isn't going to keep me quiet, so why do it?" She paused and then, with one last hope of reaching him, cried, "Go with me! Let's go together and tell them! Oh, Mark, there's got to be one place where we clear the air! Let's just go—and say how terrible it's been—and how awful we feel, how the whole thing is. Can't we?"

"No," Mark said, "we can't."

And he lit the curtain.

He lit it with a rolled newspaper that he had picked up, somehow, without Susan's noticing, from the coffee table. He touched it to the fire, and he reached across and touched it to the drapes. He held it there a moment. Despite the wind, the drapes took a little while to catch. "They're such nice, thick material," Mrs. McConnell had said, and, yes, they were that, for he held the flame at the edge for a long moment, and Susan, lying prone on the floor, watched and her throat was frozen closed so that she could say nothing. She watched the long, red splinters of fire licking at the edges of the curtains, and watched them darken and turn first brown and then black, and finally the red began on the edges, and in an instant it was leaping upward and gripping and climbing, and Susan tried to scream, but no sound came.

"You're wondering about Jeff and Betsy," Mark said. "Sure, they'll be mad, but what can they do, right? I mean, they're not in much of a position to do anything. Betsy's the one who got caught in that parking lot, with the Chevy. Jeff painted it. Nobody helped him. Anything that's happened, they're not just 'in on,' they're 'it'!" He stepped back from the flaming drapes and looked down at Susan.

"You're an okay kid," Mark said. "I never wanted anything bad to happen to you, Sue, but I never thought you'd start acting this way. When you're part of something, you can't just start switching yourself around. You know?"

The flames on the curtains were growing. Like strange, golden flowers, they were bursting into bloom, and the blossoms changed to red and orange and, once again, gold. Up, up, they climbed, and the heat was stretching itself into the room so that Susan, lying half the room away from the draperies, could feel it. Now it was licking the ceiling. What happened to ceilings when heat touched them? They began to crack. She had never asked herself such a question before, but now she did—simply because the question was there before her, and lying where she was, she could see the cracks beginning and running in sudden explosive lines away from the window, and then darkening until they looked like sections in a cake that had been placed in the oven and forgotten.

I will be burned alive, Susan thought.

But she could not believe it, because the boy standing in front of her was Mark. He was standing there, quiet, in the center of the room, and there was no longer anger on his face. His was a quiet, beautiful face, with a wide, smooth forehead, and a sweet, strong mouth, and eyes with the glow of far places and lovely dreams. I love him, Susan thought, realizing it for the first time. And I hate him. And he is going to kill me.

"Mark!" she tried to cry, but no sound came.

Mark! Susan cried in silence, Mark, help me, Mark, help me, Mark, you can't mean this, Mark, it can't be real, Mark . . . Mark . . .

But it was real, and Mark was not looking at her at all. His mind was somewhere else, in another day, at another time, and it was not this fire but another that blazed before his eyes.

"He was going to turn me in," he said softly, "his only son—his only child. The bastard was going to turn me in."

He crossed the room to the window and threw a leg across the ledge. It was in the last instant before the end of consciousness that Susan saw the two other figures standing there. The man who reached up and caught hold of Mark and yanked him out, over the sill, into the night outside.

And the woman with the stricken face.

I am going to die, Susan screamed silently, in the great, bursting consciousness that was still her mind. How else could this end, what else could ever happen?

I'm going to die, she screamed to the woman in the window. You're glad, aren't you? What else can you be but glad?

Kathy Griffin looked straight at her, and her eyes held no hatred. They were gentle, sad, accepting eyes.

I would never wish that upon you, the eyes said.

NINETEEN

Mrs. McConnell rapped lightly on the bedroom door and then opened it and entered without waiting for an answer.

"Good news, Sue," she said. "Kathy Griffin's baby was born yesterday, and it's a boy. It's in the morning paper."

"That's nice," Susan said dully.

Her mother came over and seated herself on the edge of the bed.

"Sue," she said, "you can't go on like this. It's been ten days now, and it's time you began to get yourself together. We've got to discuss what happened."

"I don't want to discuss it," Susan said. "I don't want to think about it."

"You have to. It's only by facing things that you ever put them behind you." The firmness in Mrs. McConnell's voice belied the worry in her eyes. "You've never asked why Kathy Griffin and Detective Baca came to our house that night."

"Does it matter?" Susan said.

"It certainly does. It was their coming there that saved your life. It was reading the name of Lana Turnboldt in the paper that morning that started Kathy Griffin thinking. She had heard the name the day before from Detective Baca, but she had been in such a state of shock at the time that it hadn't meant anything to her. When she read it in the paper, she realized this was the same girl who had supplied Mark Kinney with a stolen English paper, and that the 'former boyfriend' who had been with her when she discovered the picnic area by the waterfall must be he.

"She remembered she had met Mark here at our house a couple of nights before, and he had been introduced to her as a friend of yours. She knew too that you were supposedly the last person to have seen her husband alive, and she was certain you had not told the truth about the circumstances. She started putting the pieces together, and while they didn't make a complete picture, they fit well enough to raise some strong questions in her mind. She called Detective Baca and suggested that you be interviewed again, by both of them together. That's the reason they came over that evening."

"But why didn't they ring the doorbell?" Susan asked. "Why did they come around to the back of the house and look in the window?"

"They intended to ring the bell, but when they pulled up in front of our house, Kathy recognized her husband's car. You can image the effect this had on her. She was stunned. She and Detective Baca decided to circle the house and see if they could get any clue as to what was going on inside without frightening away whoever was there."

"But Jeff had painted the car," Susan said. "And Betsy changed the license plate."

"Remember, honey, it was nighttime," her mother said. "In the dark it's impossible to tell the difference between a gray car and a green one. Kathy never looked at the license plate, she looked inside the car and knew the patched upholstery. She had ridden in that car so often, there was no way she could have been fooled by a new paint job."

"Okay, now I know," Susan said. "Do we have to keep talking about it?"

"Yes," her mother said. "We need to talk about it at length with somebody who can help us understand exactly what happened to you and to the others who were under Mark's influence. Yesterday afternoon your father and I had a counseling session with a psychologist. Detective Baca recommended him to us, and we found it very helpful."

"You and Dad went to a psychologist?" Susan exclaimed, surprised out of her lethargy. "But why? There's nothing wrong with the two of you."

"You don't have to have something 'wrong with you' to need help in understanding things," Mrs. McConnell said. "Listen—I want to read you something." She drew a folded paper from her shirt pocket. "This is a description of a certain personality type."

She began to read: " 'This individual has a behavior pattern that brings him repeatedly into conflict with society. He is incapable of significant loyalty to individuals, groups or social values. He is selfish, callous, irresponsible, impulsive and totally unable to experience guilt. His frustration level is low; he cannot stand to be thwarted. He tends to blame others or offer plausible rationalizations for his behavior.' "

She paused. "Sound familiar?"

When Susan did not answer, her mother continued. "There's more. 'This individual is unique among pathological personalities in appearing, even on close examination, to be not only quite normal but unusually intelligent and charming. He appears quite sincere and loyal and may perform brilliantly at any endeavor. He often has a tremendous charismatic power over others.'

"Now, do you recognize someone?"

"It's a description of Mark," Susan said.

"It's a clinical description of a psychopath."

Susan stared at her mother. "Is that what the psychologist told you?"

"The first part of the description is a definition published by the American Psychiatric Association. The second part is paraphrased by the psychologist."

"What will be done about him?" Susan asked. "What will be done about all of us?"

"Our lawyer has requested that Mark be tried separately," Mrs. McConnell told her. "In fact, he will probably face three trials—one for his part in Brian Griffin's death, one for the possible murder of Mrs. Ruggles, and one for what he attempted to do to you. The lawyer feels that he may be able to get the charges against David, Betsy and Jeff reduced to second-degree murder. I hope he can, as that might make the difference in whether they will serve time in a prison or in a juvenile facility."

"And me?" asked Susan.

"You weren't actually involved in what took place in the mountains," Mrs. McConnell said. "That fact is in your favor. If you agree to turn state's evidence, you might be let off. The lawyer is working on that now. Otherwise, the charge will probably be manslaughter."

"Does 'turning state's evidence' mean I will have to testify against the others?"

"You will have to go on the stand and tell the

truth," her mother said. "No matter how hard it is, you will have to describe exactly what happened. Your part, and their part. Mark's part. You will have to tell it all."

"I don't think I can," Susan said.

"You can, and you must." Her mother reached over and took her hand. "You'll do whatever has to be done. Meanwhile, Dad and I think it would be a good idea to get some family counseling to help us all through this difficult time. Will you agree to that?"

"The whole family?" Susan asked.

"We're in this together, aren't we? Whatever happens to you happens to all of us. Perhaps we'll grow closer through this, somehow. Perhaps we'll all understand each other better. There must have been something lacking in our life together if you needed someone like Mark to fill in the gap."

Mrs. McConnell got to her feet, giving Susan's hand a quick squeeze before releasing it. "You've stayed in this room long enough. Get your hair combed and come downstairs. I want you to come with me when I go shopping for curtains."

"White ones?" Susan said with an effort.

"Something darker, I think. Maybe beige."

After her mother left the room, Susan sat a long time unmoving. When she rose at last it was to go over to her desk and open the top drawer. She took out an envelope and withdrew from it a sheet of lined paper.

Attached was a note:

"I found this in his briefcase. He didn't have a chance to give it back to you." It was signed, "K.G."

How long ago it seemed that she had written this final song for Ophelia. It was almost like reading a poem written by a stranger.

* * *

Where the daisies laugh and blow,
Where the willow leaves hang down,
Nonny, nonny, I will go
There to weave my lord a crown.

Willow, willow, by the brook,
Trailing fingers green and long,
I will read my lord a book,
I will sing my love a song.

Though he turn his face away,
Nonny, nonny, still I sing,
Ditties of a heart gone gray
And a hand that bears no ring.

It was the last verse that he had underlined:

Water, water, cold and deep,
Hold me fast that I may sleep.
Death with you is hardly more
Than the little deaths before.

Below this, in Mr. Griffin's small, precise handwriting, there was a message:

Miss McConnell:
 It pleases me to see the growing maturity of your work. It is indeed the "little deaths," the small, daily rejections of our well-meant offerings, that render the soul lifeless. It is an adult thought, well expressed.
 I am glad that you are a junior, for it will allow me one more year in which to work with you. I look forward to watching your continued development as a writer and hope that I may be able to contribute toward it.
                              Brian Griffin

If she had been the Susan of two weeks before, she would have wept, but this new Susan had cried herself dry of tears. She replaced the paper in the drawer and went to comb her hair.

Cassidy

Mary